All My Relations

ALL MY RELATIONS

Stories by Christopher McIlroy

The University of Georgia Press
Athens and London

Published by the University of Georgia Press
Athens, Georgia 30602
© 1994 by Christopher McIlroy

Designed by Erin Kirk
Set in Berkeley Old Style Medium by Tseng Information Systems, Inc.

The paper in this book meets the guidelines for permanence
and durability of the Committee on Production Guidelines
for Book Longevity of the Council on Library Resources.

Printed in the United States of America

Library of Congress Cataloging in Publication Data
McIlroy, Christopher.
All my relations : stories / by Christopher McIlroy.
p. cm.
ISBN 0-8203-1602-4 (alk. paper)
I. Title.
PS3563.C3689A77   1994
813'.54—dc20   93-23006

British Library Cataloging in Publication Data available

For Karen
and
for Buzz

Acknowledgments

"All My Relations" first appeared in *TriQuarterly* (Winter 1985) and was reprinted in *Best American Short Stories 1986* and in *TriQuarterly Fiction of the Eighties* (Spring/Summer 1990); "Simplifying" was first published in *TriQuarterly* (Fall 1989); "Hualapai Dread" in *Puerto del Sol* (Winter 1994); "The March of the Toys" in *Puerto del Sol* (Spring 1991); "From the Philippines" in *Sonora Review* (Spring 1984); "In a Landscape Animals Shrink to Nothing" in *Fiction* (1985); and "The Big Bang and the Good House" in *Missouri Review* (Winter 1992).

The author gratefully acknowledges the assistance of the National Endowment for the Arts, the Arizona Commission on the Arts, and the Pryor, Montana, School District.

CONTENTS

All My Relations

ALL MY RELATIONS

When Jack Oldenburg first spoke to him, Milton Enos leaned over his paper plate, scooping beans into his mouth as if he didn't hear. Breaking through the murmur of *O'odham* conversation, the white man's speech was sharp and harsh. But Oldenburg stood over him, waiting.

Oldenburg had just lost his ranch hand, sick. If Milton reported to the Box-J sober in the morning, he could work for a couple of weeks until the cowboy returned or Oldenburg found a permanent hand.

"O.K.," Milton said, knowing he wouldn't go. Earlier in the day his wife and son had left for California, so he had several days' drinking to do. Following his meal at the convenience mart he would hitch to the Sundowner Lounge at the edge of the reservation.

After a sleepless night Milton saddled his horse for the ride to Oldenburg's, unable to bear his empty house. As he crossed the wide, dry bed of the Gila River, leaving the outskirts of Hashan, the house ceased to exist for him and he thought he would never go back. Milton's stomach jogged over the pommel with the horse's easy gait. Two hours from Hashan, Oldenburg's Box-J was the only ranch in an area either left desert or irrigated for cotton and sorghum. Its twenty square miles included hills, arroyos, and the eastern tip of a mountain range—gray-pink granite knobs split by ravines. The sun burned the tops of the mountains red.

Oldenburg stood beside his corral, tall and thin as one of its mesquite logs. First, he said, sections of the barbed-wire fence had broken down, which meant chopping and trimming new posts.

Milton's first swings of the axe made him dizzy and sick. He flailed wildly, waiting with horror for the bite of the axe into his foot. But soon he gained control over his stroke. Though soft, his big arms were strong. Sweat and alcohol poured out of him until he stank.

In the afternoon Milton and Oldenburg rode the fenceline.

"Hasn't been repaired in years," Oldenburg said. "My hand Jenkins is old." Oldenburg himself was well over sixty, his crew cut white and his face dried up like a dead man's. He had bright eyes, though, and fine white teeth. Where the fence was flattened to the ground, Milton saw a swatch of red and white cowhide snagged on the barbed wire. He'd lost a few head in the mountains, Oldenburg said, and after the fence was secure they'd round them up.

"One thing I'll tell you," Oldenburg said. "You can't drink while you work for me. Alcohol is poison in a business."

Milton nodded. By reputation he knew Oldenburg had a tree stump up his ass. Milton's wife C.C. had said she'd bring their son Allen back when Milton stopped drinking. For good? he'd asked. How would she know when was for good? For all anybody knew tomorrow might be the first day of for good, or 25,000 days later he might get drunk again. For a moment Milton remembered playing Monopoly with C.C. and Allen several weekends before. As usual, Milton and Allen were winning. Pretending not to be furious, C.C. smiled her big, sweet grins. Milton and the boy imitated her, stretching their mouths, until she couldn't help laughing. Milton clicked them off like a TV set and saw only mesquite, the rocky sand, sky, and the line of fence. After his two weeks, Milton thought, he'd throw a drunk like World War Ten.

At the end of the day he accepted Oldenburg's offer: $75 a week plus room and board, weekend off. Oldenburg winced apologetically proposing the wage; the ranch didn't make money, he explained.

They ate at a metal table in the dining room. Milton, whose pleasure in food went beyond filling his stomach, appreciated Oldenburg's meat loaf—laced with onion, the center concealing three hard-boiled eggs. Milton couldn't identify the seasonings except for chili. "What's in this?" he asked.

"Sage, chili, cumin, and Worcestershire sauce."

"Heyyy."

Inside his two-room adobe, Milton was so tired he couldn't feel his body, and lying down felt the same as standing up. He slept without dreaming until Oldenburg rattled the door at daybreak.

Milton dug holes and planted posts. By noon his sweat had lost its salt and tasted like pure spring water. Then he didn't sweat at all. Chilled and shaking at the end of the day, he felt as if he'd been thrown by a horse. The pain gave him a secret exultation which he hoarded from Oldenburg, saying nothing. Yet he felt he was offering the man part of the ache as a secret gift. Slyly, he thumped his cup on the table and screeched his chair back with exaggerated vigor. Milton was afraid of liking Oldenburg too much. He liked people too easily, even those who were not *O'odham*—especially those, perhaps, because he wanted them to prove he needn't hate them.

Milton worked ten-, eleven-hour days. The soreness left his muscles, though he was as tired the fourth evening as he had been the first. Thursday night Oldenburg baked a chicken.

"You're steady," Oldenburg said. "I've seen you Pimas work hard before. What's your regular job?"

"I've worked for the government." Milton had ridden rodeo,

sold wild horses he captured in the mountains, broken horses. Most often there was welfare. Recently he had completed two CETA training programs, one as a hospital orderly and the other baking cakes. But the reservation hospital wasn't hiring, and the town of Hashan had no bakeries. For centuries, Milton had heard, when the Gila flowed, the *O'odham* had been farmers. Settlements and overgrazing upstream had choked off the river only a few generations past. Sometimes he tried to envision green plots of squash, beans, and ripening grains, watered by earthen ditches, spreading from the banks. He imagined his back flexing easily in the heat as he bent to the rows, foliage swishing his legs, finally the villagers diving into the cool river, splashing delightedly.

"I don't think Jenkins is coming out of the hospital," Oldenburg said. "This job is yours if you want it." Milton was stunned. He had never held a permanent position.

In just a week of hard work, good eating, and no drinking, Milton had lost weight. Waking Friday morning, he pounded his belly with his hand; it answered him like a drum. He danced in front of the bathroom mirror, swiveling his hips, urging himself against the sink as if it were a partner. At lunch he told Oldenburg he would spend the weekend with friends in Hashan.

When he tossed the posthole digger into the shed, he felt light and strong, as if instead of sinking fence posts he'd spent the afternoon in a deep, satisfying nap. On the way to the guest house, his bowels turned over and a sharp pain set into his head. He saw the battered station wagon rolling out the drive, C.C. at the wheel, Allen's tight face in the window.

Milton threw his work clothes against the wall. After a stinging shower, he changed and mounted his horse for the ride to Vigiliano Lopéz's.

Five hours later the Sundowner was closing. Instead of his customary beer, Milton had been drinking highball glasses of straight vodka. He felt paler and paler, like water, until he was water. His image peeled off him like a wet decal and he was only water in the shape of a man. He flowed onto the bar, hooking his water elbows onto the wooden ridge for support. Then he was lifted from the stool, tilted backward, floating on the pickup bed like vapor.

Milton woke feeling the pong, pong of a basketball bouncing outside. The vibration traveled along the dirt floor of Lopez's living room, up the couch he lay on. The sun was dazzling. Looking out the window, he saw six-foot-five, three-hundred-pound Bosque dribbling the ball with both hands, knocking the other players aside. As he jammed the ball into the low hoop, it hit the back of the rim, caroming high over the makeshift plywood backboard. A boy and two dogs chased it.

Seeing beer cans in the dirt, Milton went outside. He took his shirt off and sat against the house with a warm Bud. The lean young boys fired in jump shots, or when they missed, their fathers and older brothers pushed and wrestled for the rebound. Lopez grabbed a loose ball and ran with it, whirling for a turn-around fadeaway that traveled three feet. He laughed, and said to Milton, "When we took you home you started fighting us. Bosque had to pick you up and squeeze you, and when he did, everything came out like toothpaste."

"Try our new puke-flavored toothpaste," someone said, laughing.

"Looks like pizza."

"So we brought you here."

Milton said nothing. He watched the arms and broad backs collide. The young boys on the sidelines practiced lassoing the players' feet, the dogs, the ball. When he finished a beer, Milton started another. Later in the afternoon he sent boys to his house for the rest of his clothes and important belongings.

When the game broke up, some of the men joined the women in the shade of a mesquite. Saddling a half-broke wild colt, the boys took turns careening across the field. Lopez drove a truckload to the rodeo arena, where a bronc rider from Bapchule was practicing. Compact and muscular, with silver spurs and collar tabs, he rode out the horse's bucks, smoothing the animal to a canter. Two of Milton's drunk friends tried and were thrown immediately. For a third, the horse didn't buck but instead circled the arena at a dead run, dodging the lassos and open gates. From the announcer's booth Lopez called an imaginary race as horse and rider passed the grandstand again and again— "coming down the backstretch now, whoops, there he goes for another lap, this horse is not a quitter, ladies and gentlemen."

"Go ahead, Milton," Lopez said. "You used to ride."

Milton shook his head. Allen, thirteen, recently had graduated from steers to bulls. In both classes he had finished first or second in every start, earning as much money the past months as his father and mother combined. Would there be rodeo in California? Milton wondered. In school, too, Allen was a prodigy, an eighth grader learning high school geometry. If he studied hard, the school counselor said, he could finish high school in three years and win a college scholarship. Milton didn't know where the boy's talent came from.

Tears filled Milton's eyes.

"Aaaah," Bosque said. His big hand gripped Milton's arm. They walked back to Lopez's house and split a couple of sixes under the mesquite until the men returned. Audrey Lopez and the other wives prepared chili and *cemait* dough while the men played horseshoes and drank in the dusk.

By the end of dinner everyone was drunk. Milton, face sweating, was explaining to Audrey Lopez, "Just a few weeks ago, Allen wins some kind of puzzle contest for the whole state, O.K.? And he's on TV. And C.C. and I have got our faces up to the screen so we can hear every word he's saying. And we can't believe it. He's talking on TV, and his hair's sticking up on the side like that, just like it always does.

"I can see them so real," Milton said. "When C.C. plays volley-ball she's like a rubber ball, she's so little and round. She *dives* for those spikes, and her hair goes flying back."

Lopez slid his leg along Audrey's shoulder. "Good song," he said. "Let's dance." The radio was playing Top Forty.

"Wait. I'm listening to this man."

"Milton talks you into tomorrow afternoon. Come on." Lopez pulled her shoulder.

Audrey shrugged him off and laid her hand on Milton's arm. "His wife and son are gone."

"Dried up old bitch," Lopez said. "C.C.'s too old for you, man, she's way older than he is. You lost nothing."

Grabbing a barbecue fork, ramming Lopez against the wall, Milton chopped the fork into Lopez's shoulder. A woman screamed, Milton heard his own grunts as the glistening tines rose and stabbed. Lopez ducked and his knife came up. Milton deflected the lunge with his fork, the knife blade springing down its long shank. Milton shouted as the knife thudded into the wall. His little finger had bounded into the air and lay on the floor, looking like a brown pebble.

Bosque drove both men to the hospital. The doctor cauter-ized, stitched, and bandaged the wound, and gave Milton a tetanus shot. If Milton had brought the severed finger—the top two joints—the doctor said, he might have sewed it on. The men refused to stay overnight. When they returned to the party, couples were dancing the *choti* and *bolero* to a Mexican radio station. Gulps of vodka deadened the pain in Milton's finger. He and Lopez kept opposite corners of the living room until dawn, when Lopez pushed Audrey into Milton's arms and said, "Get some dancing, man."

Sunday Milton slept under the mesquite until evening, when he rode to the Box-J.

"That's your mistake, Milton," Oldenburg said. "Everyone's entitled to one mistake. Next time you drink you're gone. You believe me?"

Milton did. He felt like weeping. The next day he roamed the fenceline, his chest and neck clotted with the frustration of being unable to work. The horse's jouncing spurted blood through the white bandage on his finger. Finally he rode out a back gate and into the midst of the granite mountains. Past a sparkling dome broken by a slump of shattered rock, Milton trotted into a narrow cut choked with mesquite. As a boy, he would hunt wild horses for days in these ravines, alone, with only a canvas food bag tied to the saddle. He remembered sleeping on the ground without a blanket, beneath a lone sycamore that had survived years of drought. Waking as dawn lit the mountain crests, he would force through the brush, gnawing a medallion of jerked beef. Most often when he startled a horse the animal would clatter into a side gully, boxing itself in. Then roping was easy. Once when Milton flushed a stringy gray mustang, the horse charged him instead; he had no time to uncoil the rope before the gray was past. Milton wheeled, pursuing at full gallop out the canyon and onto the *bajada*. Twig-matted tail streaming behind, the mustang was outrunning him, and he had one chance with the rope. He dropped the loop around the gray's neck, jarring the animal to its haunches. It was so long ago. Today, Milton reflected, the headlong chase would have pinned him and the horse to Oldenburg's barbed-wire fence.

The sycamore held its place, older and larger. Though encountering no horses, Milton returned three stray cattle to Oldenburg's ranch. For a month, while the slightest jolt could rupture the wound, he hunted down mavericks in the miles of ravine, painted the ranch buildings, and repaired the roofs, one-handed. Even as the finger healed, the missing segment unbalanced his grip. Swinging the pick or axe, shoveling, he would clench his right hand so tightly the entire arm would tremble. By the sec-

ond month a new hand had evolved, with the musculature of
the other fingers, the palm, and the wrist more pronounced. The
pinky stub acted as a stabilizer against pickshaft or rope. Milton
had rebuilt the fence and combed the granite mountains, rounding up another two dozen head. Oldenburg's herd had increased
to 120.

In late August Milton rode beyond the granite range to the Ka
kai Mountains, a low, twisted ridge of volcanic rock that he had
avoided because he once saw the Devil there. Needing to piss,
he had stumbled away from a beer party and followed a trail
rising between the boulders. Watching the ground for snakes,
he had almost collided with a man standing in the path. The
stranger was a very big, ugly Indian, but Milton knew it was the
Devil because his eyes were black, not human, and he spoke in a
booming voice that rolled echoes off the cliff. Milton shuddered
uncontrollably and shriveled to the size of a spider. Afterwards
he found he had fallen and cut himself. Cholla spines were embedded in his leg. The Devil had said only: "Beware of Satan
within you."

The meeting enhanced Milton's prestige, and Allen was impressed, though not C.C. "You see?" she said. "What did I always
tell you?"

In daylight the mountains looked like no more than a pile of
cinders. Milton chose an arroyo that cut through the scorched
black rubble into red slabs, canyon walls that rose over his head,
then above the mesquite. Chasing a calf until it disappeared in
a side draw, Milton left the animal for later. The canyon twisted
deeper into the mountains, the red cliffs now three hundred feet
high. The polished rock glowed. Milton was twelve years old
and his brothers were fighting.

"You took my car," Steven said.

"So what," Lee said. Milton's favorite brother, he was slim and
handsome, with small ears and thick, glossy hair that fell almost
into his eyes. Weekends he took Milton into Phoenix to play

pool and pinball, sometimes to the shopping mall for Cokes. He always had girls, even Mexicans and whites.

"I told you if you took my car I was going to kill you." Steven always said crazy things. At breakfast, if Milton didn't pass him the milk right away—"How'd you like this knife in your eye?" About their mother—"Bitch wouldn't give me a dime. I'm going to shit on her bed." He wore a white rag around his head and hung out with gangs. Now they would call him a *cholo*.

"So what," Lee said. "Kill me." Cocking his leg, he wiped the dusty boot heel carefully against the couch. Milton was sitting on the couch.

Steven ran down the hall and came back with a .22. He pointed it at Lee's head, there was a shocking noise, a red spot appeared in Lee's forehead, and he collapsed on the rug.

"Oh my God," Steven said. Fingers clawed against his temples, he rushed out the door. Milton snatched the gun and chased him, firing on the run. Steven, bigger and faster, outdistanced him in the desert. Milton didn't come home for three days. Steven wasn't prosecuted and he moved to Denver. If he returned, Milton would kill him, even twenty years later.

Milton's horse ambled down the white sand, the dry bed curving around a red outcropping. Trapped by the canyon walls, the late summer air was hot and close. The weight of Milton's family fell on his back like a landslide—his father, driving home drunk from Casa Grande, slewing across the divider, head on into another pickup. The four children had flown like crickets from the back, landing unhurt in the dirt bank. The driver of the other truck died, and Milton's mother lost the shape of her face.

Milton felt himself turning to water. He circled his horse, routed the calf from the slit in the wall, and drove it miles to the ranch. At dinner he told Oldenburg he needed a trip to town.

"You'll lose your job," Oldenburg said.

Milton ate with his water fingers, spilling food and the orange juice that Oldenburg always served. "The lives of *O'odham* is a soap opera," he cried, trying to dispel his shame by insulting himself. "I love my boy, O.K.? But it's him who has to hold me when I go for C.C. He doesn't hold me with his strength. He holds me because I see him, and I stop. Sometimes I don't stop."

Oldenburg served Milton cake for dessert and told him to take the next day off if he wanted.

The following morning Milton lay on his bed, sweating. In his mind were no thoughts or images save the swirls of chill, unpleasant water that washed over him. He could transform the water, making it a cold lake that pumped his heart loudly and shrank his genitals, or a clear stream immersing him in swift currents and veins of sunlight, but he could not change the water into thoughts. The green carpeting and blue-striped drapes in his room sickened him. He could have finished a pint of vodka before he knew he was drinking.

He could not imagine losing his work.

Abruptly Milton rose. In the corral he fitted a rope bridle over the horse's head. As he rode past Oldenburg, the man looked up from a bench of tack he was fussing with, then quickly lowered his head.

"I'm going to the mountains," Milton said.

He let the horse carry him into the charred crust of the canyon. The scarlet walls rose high and sheer, closing off the black peaks beyond. Tethering the horse to a mesquite, Milton sat in the sand. The cliffs seemed almost to meet above him. Heat gathered over his head and forced down on him. A lizard skittered by his ear, up the wall. A tortoise lumbered across the wash. The water rippling through him became a shimmering on the far wall, scenes of his life. Milton racing after Steven, aiming at the zigzagging blue shirt, the crack of the gun, a palo verde trunk catching the rifle barrel and spinning Milton to his knees. His father's empty boots beside the couch where he slept. His mother in baggy gray slacks, growing fatter. C.C.'s head snapping back from Milton's open palm. The pictures flickered over the cliff. Milton sat while shadow climbed the rock, and a cool breeze funneled through the canyon, and night fell. Scooping a hole in the sand, he lay face to the stone while the canyon rustled and sighed. The wind rushed around a stone spur, scattering sand grains on his face. Several times in the night footsteps passed so near that the ground yielded beneath his head. Huddled, shivering, he thought his heart had stopped and fell asleep from terror. He dreamed of the cliffs, an unbroken glassy red.

Early in the morning Milton woke and stretched, refreshed by the cool air. The only prints beside him were his own. That evening he wrote to C.C. in care of her California aunt, telling her he'd quit drinking.

When C.C. didn't respond, Milton wrote again, asking at least for word of Allen, who would have entered high school. C.C. replied, "When I got here the doctor said I had a broken nose. Allen says he has no father."

Milton knew he must hide to avoid drinking. When he asked Oldenburg's permission to spend a day in the granite mountains, Oldenburg said he would go, too. They camped against a rock turret. The light in the sky faded and the fire leaped up. In the weeks since the former hand Jenkins's death, Oldenburg had become, if possible, more silent. Milton, meanwhile, admitted he had been a chatterbox, recalling high-school field trips to Phoenix fifteen years before, and rodeos in Tucson, Prescott, Sells, and Whiteriver. Oldenburg, fingertips joined at his chin, occasionally nodded or smiled. Tonight Milton squatted, arms around his knees, staring into the fire. About to share his most insistent emotions with the white man, he felt a giddy excitement, as if he were showing himself naked to a woman for the first time.

Milton told Oldenburg what C.C. had said.

"Your drinking has scarred them like acid. It will be time before they heal," Oldenburg said.

"There shouldn't be *O'odham* families," Milton exclaimed. "We should stop having children."

Oldenburg shook his head. After a while he said, "Milton, I hope you're not bitter because I won't let you drink. Drawing the line helps you. It's not easy living right. I've tried all my life and gained nothing—I lost both my sons in war and my wife divorced me to marry a piece of human trash. And still, in my own poor way, I try to live right." Oldenburg relaxed his shoulders and settled on his haunches.

Milton laid another mesquite limb across the fire. As the black of the sky intensified, the stars appeared as a glinting powder. Milton sipped two cups of coffee against the chill. Oldenburg, firelight sparkling off his silver tooth, wool cap pulled low over his stretched face, looked like an old grandmother. Laughing, Milton told him so. Oldenburg laughed too, rocking on his heels.

Soon after Oldenburg went to bed, Milton's mood changed. He hated the embers of the fire, the wind sweeping the rock knoll, the whirring of bats. He hated each stone and twig littering the campsite. His own fingers, spread across his knees, were like dumb, sleeping snakes. Poisonous things. He was glad one of them had been chopped off. Unrolling his blanket, he lay on his back, fists clenched. He dug hands and heels into the ground as if staked to it. After lying stiffly, eyes open, for an hour, he got up, slung his coiled rope over his shoulder, and walked down the hillside.

Brush and cactus were lit by a rising moon. Reaching a sheer drop, Milton jammed boot toes into rock fissures, seized tufts of saltbush, to let himself down. In the streambed he walked quickly until he joined the main river course. After a few miles' meandering through arroyos and over ridges, he arrived at the big sycamore and went to sleep.

Waking before dawn, Milton padded along the wash, hugging the granite. The cold morning silence was audible, a high, pure ringing. He heard the horse's snort before he saw it tearing clumps of grass from the gully bank, head tossing, lips drawn back over its yellow teeth. Rope at his hip, Milton stalked from boulder to boulder. When he stepped forward, whirling the lariat once, the horse reared, but quieted instantly as the noose tightened around its neck. Milton tugged the rope; the animal neighed and skipped backward, but followed.

During the next two days Milton and Oldenburg captured three more spindly, wiry horses. Oldenburg would flush the mustangs toward Milton, who missed only once with the lasso. The stallions Milton kept in separate pens and later sold as rodeo broncs. Within a couple of weeks he had broken the mares.

Milton consumed himself in chores. Though the Box-J was a small ranch, labor was unremitting. In the fall, summer calves were rounded up and "worked"—branded with the Box-J, castrated, and dehorned. The previous winter's calves, now some 400 to 500 pounds each, were held in sidepens for weighing and loading onto the packer's shipping trucks. The pens were so dilapidated that Milton tore them down and built new ones. Winter, he drove daily pickup loads of sorghum hay, a supplement for the withered winter grasses, to drop spots at the water holes. Oldenburg hired extra help for spring roundup, working the new winter calves. Summer, Milton roved on horseback, troubleshooting. The fenceline would need repair. Oldenburg taught him to recognize cancer-eye, which could destroy a cow's market value. A low water tank meant Oldenburg must overhaul the windmill. Throughout the year Milton inspected the herd, groomed the horses, maintained the buildings, kept tools and equipment in working order.

Certain moments, standing high in the stirrups, surveying the herd and the land which stretched from horizon to horizon as if mirroring the sky, he could believe all belonged to him.

Every two weeks, when Oldenburg drove into Casa Grande for supplies, Milton deposited half his wages—his first savings account—and mailed the rest to C.C. These checks were like money thrown blindly over the shoulder. So thoroughly had he driven his family from his mind that he couldn't summon them back, even if he wished to. When, just before sleep, spent from the day's work, he glimpsed C.C. and Allen, the faces seemed unreal. They were like people he had met and loved profoundly one night at a party, then forgotten.

The night of the first November frost, soon after the wild horse roundup, Oldenburg had asked Milton if he played cards. Milton didn't.

"Too bad," Oldenburg said. "It gets dull evenings. Jenkins and I played gin rummy. We'd go to five thousand, take us a couple of weeks, and then start again."

"We could cook," Milton said.

On Sunday he and Oldenburg baked cakes. Milton missed the pressurized frosting cans with which he'd squirted flowers and desert scenes at the CETA bakery, but Oldenburg's cherry-chocolate layer cake was so good he ate a third of it. Oldenburg complimented him on his angel food.

Oldenburg bought a paperback *Joy of Cooking* in Casa Grande. Though he and Milton had been satisfied with their main dishes, they tried Carbonnade Flamande, Chicken Paprika, Quick Spaghetti Meat Pie. Milton liked New England Boiled Dinner. Mostly they made desserts. After experimenting with mousses and custard, they settled on cakes—banana, golden, seed, sponge, four-egg, Lady Baltimore, the Rombauer Special. Stacks of foil-wrapped cakes accumulated in the freezer. The men contributed cakes to charitable bake sales. Milton found that after his nightly slab of cake sleep came more easily and gently.

The men were serious in the kitchen. Standing side by side in white aprons tacked together from sheets, Milton whisking egg whites, Oldenburg drizzling chocolate over pound cake, they would say little. Milton might ask the whereabouts of a spice; Oldenburg's refusal to label the jars irritated him. Then they sat by the warm stove, feet propped on crates, and steamed themselves in the moist smells.

As they relaxed on a Sunday afternoon, eating fresh, hot cake,

Oldenburg startled Milton by wondering aloud if his own wife were still alive. She had left him in 1963, and they'd had no contact since their second son was killed in 1969, more than ten years before.

"She wanted a Nevada divorce," Oldenburg said, "but I served papers on her first, and I got custody of the boys. I prevented a great injustice." He had sold his business in Colorado and bought the ranch. "The boys hated it," he said. "They couldn't wait to join the Army."

In Hashan, Milton said, she and her lover would have been killed.

Oldenburg shook his head impatiently. "He's deserted her, certainly. He was a basketball coach, and much younger than she was."

A Pima phrase—he knew little Pima—occurred to Milton. *Ne ha: jun*—all my relations. "Here is the opposite," Milton said. "We should call this the No-Relations Ranch."

Oldenburg sputtered with laughter. "Yes! And we'd need a new brand. Little round faces with big X's over them."

"You'd better be careful. People would start calling it the Tic-tac-toe Ranch."

"Or a manual, you know, a sex manual, for fornication. The X's doing it to the O's."

Light-headed from the rich, heavily-frosted cake, they sprayed crumbs from their mouths, laughing.

At the Pinal County Fair in May, Oldenburg entered a walnut pie and goaded Milton into baking his specialty, a jelly roll. It received honorable mention, while Oldenburg won second prize.

Milton wrote C.C., "I'm better than a restaurant."

C.C. didn't answer. When Valley Bank opened a Hashan branch in June, Milton transferred his account and began meeting his friends for the first time in a year. They needled him, "Milton, you sleeping with that old man?" His second Friday in town, Milton was writing out a deposit slip when he heard Bosque say, "Milton Oldenburg."

"Yes, Daddy just gave him his allowance," said Helene Mashad, the teller.

Bosque punched him on the shoulder and put out his hand. Milton shook it, self-conscious about his missing finger.

Bosque was cashing his unemployment check. The factory where he'd manufactured plastic tote bags for the past six months had closed. "Doesn't matter," Bosque said. "I'm living good." Before leaving, he said to come on by.

"You know what Oldenburg's doing, don't you?" Helene said, smoothing the wrinkles from Milton's check. She still wore her long, lavender Phoenix nails and a frothy perm. After years in Phoenix she'd relocated at the new branch, closer to her home in Black Butte. "Oldenburg wants to marry you. Then he'll get some kind of government money for his Indian wife. Or he'll adopt you. Same deal."

"It's not me who's the wife or child. I run that place." Nervous speaking to a woman again, Milton rambled, boasting of his authority over hired crews, what Oldenburg called his quick mind and fast hands cutting calves or constructing a corner brace, his skill with new tools. Even his baking. "He has to be the wife," Milton said. "He's a better cook." Milton leaned his hip against the counter. "Older woman. He's so old he turned white. And he lost his shape." Milton's hands made breasts. "Nothing left."

They both laughed. Elated by the success of his joke, Milton asked her to dinner. Helene said yes, pick her up at six.

Milton was uneasy in Hashan. The dusty buildings—adobes, sandwich houses of mud and board, slump-block tract homes— seemed part of the unreal life that included his family. To kill time, he rode to the trading post in Black Butte, a few miles in the direction of Oldenburg's ranch, and read magazines. When he arrived at the bank, Helene slapped her forehead: she hadn't known he was on horseback. Phew, she said, she didn't want to go out with a horse. Milton should follow her home and take a bath first.

They never left her house. She was eager for him, and Milton realized that as a man he'd been dead for a year. They made love until early morning. Milton lay propped against the headboard, his arm encircling her, her cheek resting on his chest. She briskly stroked his hand.

"Your poor finger," she said. "I hear Lopez has little circles in his shoulder like where worms have gone into a tomato."

"It was bad," Milton said, closing his hand.

"I can't stand the men in this town, the drunken pigs," Helene said. "I don't know why I came back."

Helene wasn't what Milton wanted, but he liked her well enough to visit once or twice a month. Because she lived outside Hashan, few people knew of the affair. They would eat dinner and see a movie in Casa Grande or Phoenix, and go to bed. Sometimes they simply watched TV in bed, or drove Helene's Toyota through the desert, for miles without seeing another light.

When Milton returned from his second weekend with Helene, Oldenburg was peevish. "You drink with that woman?" he said. "You going to send her picture to your wife?" Emergencies arose that kept Milton on the ranch weekends. After selling two wild colts to a stable, he took Helene to Phoenix overnight. Oldenburg berated him, "The cows don't calve on Saturday and Sunday? They don't get sick? A shed doesn't blow down on Sunday?" Still the men baked together. At the beginning of the school year they entered a fund-raising bakeoff sponsored by the PTO. Oldenburg won first with a Boston cream pie, and Milton's apple ring took second.

Helene transferred to Casa Grande, and Milton brought his account with her, relieved to avoid Hashan. Conversations with his friends were strained and dead. He worked; they didn't. They drank; he didn't. They had families. Milton nodded when he saw them, but no longer stopped to talk.

Fridays after Helene punched out, they might browse in the Casa Grande shopping center. Milton was drawn to the camera displays, neat lumps of technology embedded in towers of colorful film boxes. The Lerner shop's manikins fascinated him— bony stick figures like the bleached branches of felled cottonwood, a beautiful still arrangement. "Imagine Pimas in those," Helen said, pointing to the squares and triangles of glittering cloth. She puffed out her cheeks and spread her arms. Milton squeezed her small buttocks. Helene's legs were the slimmest of any *O'odham* woman he'd known.

During the second week of October, when Milton and a hired crew had set up shipping pens and begun culling the calves, a rare fall downpour, tail end of a Gulf hurricane, struck. For six hours thunder exploded and snarls of lightning webbed the sky. The deluge turned the ground to slop, sprang leaks in the roof, and washed out the floodgates at the edge of the granite mountains. Cattle stampeded through the openings; one died, entangled in the barbed wire. When the skies cleared, Oldenburg estimated that a quarter of the cash animals, some three hundred dollars apiece, had escaped. The shipping trucks were due in two days.

The next morning a new hired man brought further news: over the weekend a fight had broken out at the Sundowner. The fat end of a pool cue had caught Audrey Lopez across the throat, crushing her windpipe. Her funeral was to be at two in the afternoon.

Milton stood helplessly before Oldenburg. In the aftermath of the storm the sky was piercingly blue and a bracing wind stung his cheeks. Oldenburg's collar fluttered.

"You have to go," Oldenburg said. "There's no question."

"You'll lose too much money," Milton said stubbornly. "The cattle are in the mountains and I know every little canyon where they run."

"There's no question," Oldenburg repeated. "The right way is always plain, though we do our best to obscure it."

The service took place in a small, white Spanish-style church. At the cemetery the mourners stood bareheaded, the sun glinting off their hair. The cemetery was on a knoll, and in the broad afternoon light the surrounding plains, spotted by occasional cloud shadows, seemed immensely distant, like valleys at the foot of a solitary butte. Milton imagined the people at the tip of a rock spire miles in the clouds. The overcast dimmed them, and shreds of cumulus drifted past their backs and bowed heads.

Afterwards the men adjourned to the Lopez house, where Vigiliano Lopez rushed about the living room, flinging chairs aside to clear a center space. A ring of some twenty men sat on chairs or against the wall. Bosque arrived carrying three cold cases and two quarts of Crown Russe. More bottles appeared. Lopez started one Crown Russe in each direction and stalked back and forth from the kitchen, delivering beer and slapping bags of potato chips at the men's feet.

At his turn, Milton passed the bottle along.

"Drink, you goddamn Milton Oldenburg," Lopez said.

Milton said, "I'll lose my job."

"So?" Lopez shrugged distractedly. "I haven't had a job in a year. I don't need a job." Lopez had been the only Pima miner at the nearby Loma Linda pit until Anaconda shut it down. He pushed his hair repeatedly off his forehead, as if trying to remember something, then turned up the radio.

Milton sat erect in the chair, hands planted on his knees. He gobbled the potato chips. No one avoided him, nor he anyone else, yet talk was impossible. Grief surged through the party like a wave. Milton felt it in the over-loud conversation, silences, the restlessness—no one able to stay in one place for long. Laughter came in fits. Over the radio, the wailing tremolos of the Mexican ballads were oppressive and nerve-wracking. The power of feeling in the room moved Milton and frightened him, but he was outside it.

Joining the others would be as simple as claiming the vodka

bottle on its next round, Milton knew. But he remembered standing tall in the stirrups, as if he could see over the edge of the yellow horizon, the end of Oldenburg's land, and he kept his hands spread on his knees. At the thought of vodka's sickly tastelessness, bile rose in his throat. Pretending to drink, tipping the bottle and plugging it with his tongue, would be foolish and shameful. Out of friendship and respect for Lopez, he could not leave. Their wounding each other, Milton realized, had bound him more closely to Lopez.

As night fell the men became drunker and louder. Bosque went out for more liquor. When he returned, he danced with the oil-drum cookstove, blackening his hands and shirt.

"Hey, not with my wife," Lopez said, grabbing the drum and humping it against the wall. "Need somebody to do you right, baby," he said. The drum clanged to the floor. The men cheered. Lopez, knees bent and hands outstretched as if waiting for something to fall into them, lurched to the middle of the room. A smile was glazed over his face. He saw Milton.

"Drink with me, you son of a bitch," he shouted.

Milton motioned for the Crown Russe, a third full. "Half for you, half for me," he said. Marking a spot on the label with his finger, Milton drank two long swallows and held out the bottle for Lopez. Lopez drank and flipped the empty over his shoulder. Side by side, arms around each other, Milton and Lopez danced the *cumbia*. Lopez's weight sagged until Milton practically carried him. The man's trailing feet hooked an extension cord, sending a lamp and the radio crashing to the floor. Lopez collapsed.

Milton ran outside and retched. Immediately he was refreshed and lucid. The stars burned like drillpoints of light. Patting the horse into an easy walk, he sat back in the saddle, reins loose in his lap, and gave himself to the brilliant stillness. As his eyes adjusted to the night, he could distinguish the black silhouettes of mountains against the lesser dark of the sky. Faint stars emerged over the ranges, bringing the peaks closer. The mountains were calm and friendly, even the jagged line of the Ka kai.

That night Milton dreamed that a chocolate-colored flood swept through Hashan. The *O'odham* bobbed on the foam; from the shore others dove backward into the torrent, arms raised symmetrically by their heads. Receding, the flood left bodies swollen in the mud—Milton's brother Lee, their mother, belly down, rising in a mound. Milton, long hair fixed in the mud, stared upward. His hands were so full of fingers they had become agaves, clusters of fleshy, spiny leaves. Peering down at him, C.C. and Allen were black against the sun, arms crooked as if for flight. Milton was glad they had escaped.

Milton woke serene and energetic, the dream forgotten. Over breakfast Oldenburg studied him intently—clear gray eyes, a slight frown—but said nothing. The penned calves were weighed and loaded onto the shipping trucks. Many remained free, and the year would be a loss.

Milton wrote C.C. of Audrey Lopez's death. "I had a big drink to keep Lopez company," he added, "but I threw it up. It was the first booze in more than a year. I don't like it any more."

Lying beside Milton the following weekend, Helene said, "Poor finger. I'll give you another one." She laid her pinky against the stub so a new finger seemed to grow. Her lavender nail looked like the fancy gem of a ring. She lifted, lowered the finger. "And Lopez with the purple spots on his shoulder like the eyes of a potato," she said. She shifted and her small, hard nipple brushed Milton's side. "It's a wonder you two didn't fight."

"Shut up," Milton said. "His wife is dead."

"I know. It's terrible." She had worried for him, Helene said, knowing he would be at the funeral with Lopez. He should have brought her.

"I didn't want you there," Milton said. "You don't have the right feelings." He left before dawn and hadn't returned to Helene when C.C. replied.

"I was shocked to hear about Audrey," C.C. wrote. "I feel sad about it every day. Hashan is such a bad place. But it isn't any better here. At Allen's school there are gangs and not just Mexicans but black and white too."

She wrote again: "I miss you. I've been thinking about coming back. Allen says he won't but he'll come with me in the end. The money has helped. Thank you."

Milton threw up his arms and danced on the corral dirt, still moist and reddened from fluke autumn rains. Shouting, he danced on one leg and the other, dipping from side to side as if soaring, his head whirling. Oldenburg's nagging—where will they live?—worried him little. Over dinner Oldenburg suggested, "They'll live in your old place, and you can visit them on weekends. We'll have to move our baking to the middle of the week."

Milton knew he must be with the *O'odham*. Announcing a ride into the mountains, he saddled up and galloped toward Hashan. Because he couldn't see the faces of his family, his joy felt weirdly rootless. The past year he had killed them inside. The sudden aches for Allen, the sensation of carrying C.C.'s weight in his arms, had been like the twinges of heat, cold, and pain from his missing finger. As if straining after their elusive faces, Milton rode faster. His straw hat, blown back and held by its cord, flapped at his ear. The horse's neck was soaked with sweat.

Bosque's fat wife said he wasn't home. Milton made a plan for the Sundowner: after one draft for sociability, he would play the shuffleboard game. Tying up at a light pole, he hesitated in the lounge doorway. The familiarity of the raw wood beams criss-crossing the bare Sheetrock walls frightened him. But Bosque, sliding his rear off a barstool, called, "Milton Oldenburg."

"C.C.'s hauling her little tail home," Milton announced. "And the boy."

"All riiight." Bosque pumped his hand up and down. Milton's embarrassment at his missing finger disappeared in the vastness of Bosque's grip. Friends he hadn't spoken to in months surrounded him. "When's she coming? She going to live on the ranch? Oldenburg will have a whole Indian family now." Warmed by their celebration of his good luck, Milton ordered pitchers. His glass of draft was deep gold and sweeter than he had remembered, though flat. Others treated him in return. Someone told a story of Bosque building a scrap wood raft to sail the shallow lake left by the rains. Halfway across, the raft had broken apart and sunk. "Bosque was all mud up to his eyes," the storyteller said. "He looked like a bull rolling in cow flop." Everyone laughed.

Fuzzy after a half dozen beers, Milton felt his heart pound, and his blood. He saw them then—C.C., wings of hair, white teeth, dimpled round cheeks. Allen's straight bangs and small, unsmiling mouth. Their eyes were black with ripples of light, reflections on a pool. Milton was drawn into that pool, lost. Terror washed over him like a cold liquid, and he ordered a vodka.

"I'm a drunk," he told the neighbor on his right.

"Could be. Let's check that out, Milton," the man said.

"I never worked."

"No way," the man said, shaking his head.

"I didn't make a living for them."

"Not even a little bitty bit," the man agreed.

"Not even this much," Milton said, holding his thumb and forefinger almost closed, momentarily diverted by the game. "I hurt them."

Holding up his hands, the man yelled, "Not me."

"I tortured them. They don't belong to me. I don't have a family," Milton mumbled. Quickly he drank three double vodkas. The jukebox streamed colors, and he floated on its garbled music.

Shoving against the men's room door, Milton splashed into the urinal, wavering against the stall. He groped for the Sundowner's rear exit. The cold bit through his jacket. He pitched against a stack of bricks.

Waking in the dark, Milton jumped to his feet. C.C. was coming, and his job was in danger. He was foreman of a white man's ranch. Allen and C.C. would be amazed at his spread. With a bigger bank account than three-quarters of Hashan, he could support them for a year on savings alone. The night before was an ugly blur. But his tongue was bitter, his head thudded, he had the shakes. Cursing, Milton mounted and kicked the horse into a canter. To deceive Oldenburg he must work like a crazy man and sweat out his hangover. The fits of nausea made him moan with frustration. He kicked the horse and struck his own head.

Milton arrived an hour after sunup. Shooing the horse into the corral with a smack to the rump, he stood foggily at the gate, unable to remember his chore from the previous day. A ladder leaning against the barn reminded him: patching. He lugged a roll of asphalt roofing up the ladder. Scrambling over the steep pitch didn't frighten him, even when he slipped and tore his hands. He smeared tar, pressed the material into place, drove the nails. Every stroke was true, two per nail. Milton had laid half a new roof when Oldenburg called him.

"Come down." Oldenburg was pointing to the corral. The gate was still ajar. Milton's horse, head drooping, dozed against the rail, but the other three were gone.

Milton stood before him, wobbly from exertion, blood draining from his head.

"You lied," Oldenburg said. "You abandoned your job. The week is *my* time. You've been drunk. I'm going to have to let you go, Milton."

Milton couldn't speak.

"You understand, don't you?" Oldenburg said more rapidly.

His eyes flicked down, back to Milton. "Do you see what happens?" His arms extended toward the empty corral.

"So I lose a day running them down."

Smiling slightly, Oldenburg shook his head. "You miss the point. It would be wrong for me to break my word. You'd have no cause to believe me again and our agreement would be meaningless."

"Once a year I get drunk," Milton burst out. "We'll put a name on it, November Something Milton's Holiday."

Oldenburg smiled again. "Once a month . . . once a week . . . I'm sorry. I'll give you two weeks' pay but you can leave any time." He turned.

"I've worked hard for you!" Milton's throat felt as if it were closing up.

Oldenburg stopped, brow furrowed. "It's sad," he said. "You've managed the Box-J better than I could. I'm going to miss our baking." He paused. "But we have to go on, Milton, don't you see? My family leaves me, Jenkins leaves me, you leave me. But *I* go on." He walked away.

Two long steps, a knee in the back, arms around the neck, and he could break the man in half—Milton's arms dropped. He had lost the urge for violence. Long after Oldenburg had disappeared into the open green range where the horses were, he stood by the corral. Then, arms over his head as if escaping a cloudburst, he ran into the adobe, packed his belongings in a sheet, and that afternoon rode the exhausted horse back to his old home.

To C.C., Milton wrote, "I don't have my job any more but there's plenty of money in the bank." Weeks later she replied, "Milton, I know what's going on. I can't come home to this." But she would continue to write him, she said. Milton saw no one. Pacing the house, he talked to the portraits over the TV— Allen's eighth-grade class picture, a computer-drawn black-dot

composition of C.C. from the O'odham Tash carnival. He dis-
turbed nothing, not even the year-and-a-half-old pile of dishes
in the sink.

For several weeks he laid fence for a Highway Maintenance
heavy equipment yard. Working with a new type of fence, chain
link topped with barbed wire, cheered him. The foreman was
lax, married to one of Milton's cousins, so when Milton requested the leftover spools of barbed wire, he said, "Sure. It's
paid for."

Milton dug holes around his house and cut posts from the
warped, gnarled mesquite growing in the vacant land. As he
worked, the blue sky poured through chinks in the posts, reminding him pleasantly of the timeless first days repairing the
line on Oldenburg's range. When he had finished stringing the
wire, Milton's house was enclosed in a neat box—two thorned
strands, glinting silver. Sunlight jumped off the metal in zigzag
bolts. In Hashan, where fences were unknown and the beige
ground was broken only by houses, cactus, and drab shrubs,
the effect was as startling as if Milton had wrapped his home in
Christmas lights.

Milton sat on the back doorstep, drinking beer. Discouraged
by the fence, no one visited at first. But dogs still ran through
the yard, as did children, who preferred scaling the fence to
slithering under it. Their legs waggled precariously on the stiffly
swaying wire; then they hopped down, dashed to the opposite
side, and climbed out, awkward as spiders. Milton's fence became a community joke, which made him popular. Instead of
walking through the gap behind the house, friends would crawl
between the strands or try to vault them. Or they would lean on
the posts, passing a beer back and forth while they chatted.

Keeping her promise, C.C. wrote that Allen had shot up tall.
Even running track he wore his Walkman, she said. But he
smoked, and she had to yell at him. Last term he'd made nearly
all A's.

Milton grew extremely fat, seldom leaving the house except to shop or work the odd jobs his new skills brought him. Through spring and summer he drowsed on the doorstep. In November, almost a year after he'd left Oldenburg's, he fell asleep on the concrete slab and spent the night without jacket or blanket. The next day he was very sick, and Bosque and Lopez drove him to the hospital. The doctor said he had pneumonia.

Milton's first day in ICU, Bosque and Lopez shot craps with him during visiting hours. But as his lungs continued to fill with fluids, his heart, invaded by fatty tissues from his years of drinking, weakened. Four days after entering the hospital, he suffered a heart attack.

In the coronary ward, restricted to ten-minute visits, Milton dreamed, feeling as if the fluids had leaked into his skull and his brain was sodden. In one dream the agaves again sprouted from his wrists, their stalks reaching into the sky. He gave the name *ne ha: jun*—all my relations—to his agave hands.

The next morning C.C. and Allen appeared in the doorway. Huge, billowing, formless as smoke, they approached the bed in a peculiar rolling motion. Milton was afraid. From the dreams he realized that his deepest love was drawn from a lake far beneath him, and that lake was death. But understanding, he lost his fear. He held out his arms to them.

Simplifying

Easter morning Julia was dressed for church, watering her plants, when the air left her, as if her chest, while straining to expand, had flattened. From her knees she dialed 911.

The oxygen mask was a fuzzy lump in her field of vision. White-jacketed EMT's circled her. At Emergency her gurney flew down the corridor.

Her son Tim stood over the bed, hair awry, shirttail untucked. He squeezed her hand.

After visiting hours the busy noises ceased, replaced by the wheezing of therapeutic machinery, the bellows-like breaths of hospital maintenance systems, punctuated by rhythmic groans of a patient across the hall. Uniform gray light left objects distinct but without relation to each other. Certain her breath would stop if she slept, Julia remained vigilant.

Since the moment was unendurable, she chose another— Tim's first apprehension of her, not as food or warmth, but a person, age four months. She had been swinging him in his canvas pouch. With his every downward swoop she reared back, hands upraised, in open-mouthed astonishment. Tim's laughing shriek squinted his eyes and showed his pink gums. But then he simply stared at her, I know you, you wonderful being. For two or three passes they beamed at each other.

The gray set around her again, like gelatin.

"All this brouhaha for someone who's dying," she said to the nurses and technicians who monitored and tested her the next morning.

No, the doctor insisted. Although bronchitis had degenerated into emphysema, her most acute symptoms were anxiety and fatigue. "You will never lose this disease, and it will shorten your life, but we're talking years," he said. Unless she continued to smoke. "Then you might as well hop under a bus."

"Stay with me tonight," she told Tim.

He fussed. "Against hospital regulations. I'm not a whatcha-macallit, garlic around the neck for vampires, a talisman."

"Make an effort," Julia said.

Tim arranged a bed of chairs beside her, and she slept. Within a week prednisone had stabilized respiration and she was discharged.

When Julia stepped into her townhouse, even the gaudy Persian carpet was stale with her confinement. She had been ill for months before hospitalization. Nothing had changed except she wasn't coughing. She would watch PBS and attend theater and symphony with her reliable friends. Tim would appear at metronomically paced intervals. The current agreement was once every three weeks.

Julia tried to organize a routine. Retired two years, she was a zoo docent, but the connection had lapsed. Phoning booked her three days in the zoo's information booth.

Paying for groceries at the supermarket checkout, she yearned for a cigarette, that perfect moment when the body relaxed, the smoke jetted through mouth and throat to the lungs, out the nose, a continuity, complete. At even the crinkle of a package in her hand she was swollen with fondness like an escaped balloon. She bought Carltons.

Lighting the cigarette she hyperventilated and it burned halfway before she could inhale. She sipped experimentally, drew more deeply. After fifty-three years of a carton a week, she must retrain herself to smoke.

Sunday, when the Unitarian congregation volunteered personal announcements, a man named Philip said, "I love to cook, but there's no one but myself to enjoy it." He wanted to exchange dinners. A newcomer, he was six and a half feet tall, with a beard like fleece to his chest. He wore a gold earring.

To Julia the moment presented itself as a question: Am I acting for my life or against it? She felt she existed only through what she did. She stood. "I'd like that, too," she said. They agreed on the following Saturday.

Since her husband's death six years before, Julia hadn't dated, not from deference—they had been divorced sixteen years—but simply believing that whole business was over. Saturday she chose a heavy cotton smock, jungle green threaded with scarlet and yellow. She even brushed on makeup.

Philip's second-floor apartment was one room with bath and kitchenette, walls bare. Though he had lived there two years, stacked books occupied the floor, crowding desk and futon into a corner.

Philip's meal consisted of thin-sliced abalone stir-fried with vegetables, and fat black mushrooms like those unspeakable sea-bottom creatures that one tried to accept as equal living things. The whole was drenched in chili oil.

Cross-legged on a mat, they ate from bowls. The food scalded Julia's mouth and flushed her skin. Their eyes teared, faces dripping sweat. Rocking, they laughed at the ridiculous agony.

"I'll never eat anything like this again," Julia said. "Whoops, no, give me the recipe and I'll cook it for my son. Just kidding."

"He lives with you?"

Julia explained the schedule, one visit every three weeks, that Tim had dictated.

"Grotesque," Philip said. "A crueler deprivation than absence altogether."

"No. At least I have him this much."

Philip was childless. "For my wife and me, making a baby would have implied too much optimism about our future," he said.

Tim was an only. "Opportunities for conception in my marriage were rare," Julia said lightly, but again her face burned. She had decided to hold back nothing from Philip. "If we're going to be friends, I don't want to offer myself under false pretenses. I've been through a difficult episode."

"Oh?"

Since childhood Julia's sicknesses inexorably progressed to bronchitis. "I can't sleep with your barking all night," her father had told her. Every winter, for two or three weeks, a month, coughing from a chest cold interrupted conversation, eating, and her job as a home visitor for D.E.S. She canceled outings with friends.

The past November a tickle in her throat descended to her lungs. For five months the cough flapped her like a rag. Sleepless at night, Julia fell into afternoon naps on the couch. Without appetite, she drank soup. By Easter catches occurred in her breathing, when the ribcage would lift, diaphragm push— finally, whistling, a shallow expansion of the lungs.

Bent, hacking, Julia felt inescapably herself. Her shame at the noise, helpless jerking, sputum balled in Kleenex, was linked to the profounder embarrassments: her husband locked in the study with vodka and the Sons of the Pioneers. Tim accusing her, "You give me a *Peanuts* cartoon book, and when I don't laugh you say I've lost my sense of humor. *Your* sense of humor. When I'm with you I have to make a mental checklist of who I am."

Embarrassment alone could make her cough, knocking the air out of her.

Julia had begun smoking in boarding school, where the girls called their cigs "little man," as in "I have a rendezvous on the balcony with little man." Beyond this delicious intimacy, Julia's cigarette was a complete if momentary satisfaction, a devotion to wholeness in things, the opposite of embarrassment. Of course it aggravated the cough.

As she concluded with her release from the hospital, Philip wrapped her in his arms. "Poor Julia."

"That's not what I meant," she said, but his broad hands cradled her back, and she settled into his embrace as if it received her exhaustion, not only from the recitation, but the months themselves. Philip straightened his legs to give her a lap. Smelling him through the faintly soapy denim shirt, Julia lay without speaking until, nearly asleep, she said, "I've got to go."

Philip was unavailable the next weekend, so they set Thursday before, at her place.

When he arrived, Julia suggested a turn around the zoo. The coq au vin she had stewed the previous night; it needed only reheating. The park was so near her townhouse that nights she heard whooping, roaring, and trumpeting. May was still spring, temperature 85, and evening shaded the paths. Philip strode leisurely, hands in pockets, head swiveling with curiosity. In the aviary his eyes, intent, enlarged comically, tracking parrots' arrows of color.

"Why don't I do this?" he said. "The air is marvelous. I never go out."

Julia chirped to the elephant. Swaying toward them, it greeted her with raised trunk.

"Julia, Dame of the Beasts," Philip said.

"This is Philip," Julia said. "Let's see, we toured the cat enclosures, and the lions were asleep, but the tiger was swimming,
which I've never seen before." His flanks had dripped, the sheen
of his coat red-gold.

The elephant slapped its trunk side to side, head down, in
cadence with Julia's voice.

"That great head with its ludicrous tweak of hair. The animal is so unselfconscious," Philip said. "What separates them
from us," he muttered. "But not you. You don't seem to formulate
yourself for the world."

Quickly Julia skirted the sun bears, who, still awaiting their
promised habitat, paced the cage, thrusting reproachful noses.

"For all that I love the tiger," she said, "and the elephant—and
the otters—and the polar bears—and the birds"—she laughed
—"I keep coming back to the monkeys." The macaques showed
their gums and launched into a dizzying orbit of stump, trapeze,
and bars.

Leaping for an overhanging mesquite branch, Philip swung
one-armed, grinning. His teeth were weathered like piano keys.
The plummet of feeling about him, not yet for him, filled Julia
with dread.

Though landing softly, Philip winced.

"You're quiet," Julia said presently.

"My feet." His gait became delicate. "According to the doctor,
heaving around my bulk all these years has jumbled the bones.
Like a paleontological dig, fossils heaped up. I like to think
that the burden has left the bones sad, disoriented. Anomie has
set in."

"That's the most highly developed thought about anyone's feet
that I've heard."

He laughed. "Curse of my life."

Sunset ignited the haze of dust over the veldt herds. In the
fullness of the moment Julia opened her purse for a cigarette—

she'd kept a half-pack daily limit—but imagined Philip's exclamation, "Emphysema?" Idiotic, she agreed, abashed as if he'd actually spoken, and withdrew her hand.

At the dinner table Julia fork-separated the tender chicken, but Philip ate with his fingers, gray sauce running into his beard, bones protruding like catfish barbels beyond his face.

"You look like an amiable sea monster," she said.

"Mmm." He seized her hand and nibbled up her arm. She scrunched back in her chair.

Rising, stooping over her, Philip lifted Julia in his arms until she stood tight against him. His heartbeat accelerated by her ear.

Julia's hands pushed against his chest. "Not yet."

But when?

Julia poised on the deck of the community pool. Since her hospitalization the mere thought of swimming, the labored breaths, had constricted her chest. Now she craved the churning of arms and legs, the euphoric fatigue.

Julia had not made love as an old body. To conceal loosening skin she wore garments to her wrists and ankles. For occasional dips, always at night, she'd hiked panty hose under her suit. But this shyness would not lessen with waiting. Refusing Philip now, she understood, would be final.

Floodlights fanned a seething blue across the pool's surface. Beneath, the water was black, leaves circling. Julia would be diving into her own shadow, a thought she found unnerving and recklessly pleasurable. She splashed in, stroking easily.

When she and Philip undressed, Julia was compelled to imagine herself through his hands—skin sagging from the bone, flesh shrunken—and she could not respond.

Driving home in lemony brightness, Mother's Day, she resigned herself to not seeing Philip again. The affair already was a gift, more than she'd expected from her life. She memorized, for the future, Philip's trunk of a body at the window, arms spread, sunlight playing over chest and belly hair.

Awaiting her guests, Julia felt acute but out of control, like a clear-headed drunk whose body consistently lurches into furniture. She drilled the vacuum cleaner into a spot of ground dirt by the entranceway.

Two weeks before as an amendment to Julia's celebration, Tim had requested including his new girlfriend, Linda.

"Come yourself on Saturday then, for lunch," Julia had said.

Recognizing the ploy, an extra visit, Tim hesitated.

"Mother's Day is a freebie," Julia said.

Tim blushed. "Sure."

"I've had two dinner dates."

"Wow. Congratulations." The burden of her affections visibly slid from his shoulders.

"He's a poet but looks like a pirate. Gilbert and Sullivan, pirate and pilot."

"Apprentice to a pi-rate," Tim had sung, surprisingly. *Penzance* was a childhood enthusiasm.

Julia had sung a verse. "I'll put it on," she said, starting for the records.

"No, that's O.K.," Tim had said.

Julia stuffed the vacuum in the closet just as Tim arrived with steaks and Linda, a woman with flat, functional hands and a stupendous bust restrained by a snug flowered jump suit.

"What a relief," Linda said, admiring the lace-embroidered bodice of Julia's blouse. "I was afraid I'd overdressed." She and Tim were dancing later, she explained.

"Tim might not remember, but he's always been a dancer," Julia said. The blunder loomed, yet she couldn't fend off the words. "Until he was seven or eight we would dance naked together, Shostakovitch, running up and down with scarves."

"Great." Tim flipped his hands. "Now tell her how I breast-fed until I was twenty."

But Tim, who honored holidays, righted himself, telling amusing work stories. He was Target's store manager.

Through dinner Julia's stomach still clenched from his anger. "Katherine," she said, "could you pour me more wine while you're up?" Katherine was Linda's predecessor, and Julia's favorite, in Tim's succession of women.

"Mom!"

"I'm sorry. Linda. It's habit."

"I understand." Linda smiled as if to gobble the world's unhappiness, bite by bite. "Your vinaigrette was delicious." She complimented each course in detail, wielding praise like an iron over a wrinkled shirt.

The pie was heated. Linda chatted through hers, Julia dawdled, Tim ate silently and quickly. Utensils clicked on the plates. The scraped-clean surfaces gleamed as if the evening had disappeared into them. Pressure built in Julia's chest. She gasped and swallowed air.

"I bought Kahlua," she said.

No, they said, the club already would be crowded.

At the doorway Linda kissed Julia thanks, twined her arm around Tim's waist. Solitary, Julia felt conspicuous, as if the others were ignoring a comical deformity, hands sewn on the wrong wrists maybe. "Tim, I almost forgot," she said. "I've organized my papers in a filing cabinet, insurance, the will, investments, taxes. Alphabetized. It'll only take a minute. You must know, in case anything happens to me. Much as we want to avoid the fact, I am ill."

"Mom, good God, not on Mother's Day."

By 10:30 Julia had smoked her daily quota. The pact with herself was inviolable. Instead she watched a Cary Grant double feature. Cary waltzed and feinted through the heroine's amorous lunges as if greased. At midnight Julia lit #1 for the following day.

She awoke with what she thought was a severe hangover, though she had drunk moderately. After phoning in sick to the zoo she returned to bed with the blinds drawn, a shirt over her eyes. She saw Philip turning from the window, approaching, nothing between them but the sheet drawn to her chin. Cigarettes tasted like smoldering chemicals and made her head throb. She wasn't aware when night fell. The next day was no better, so, she decided, there was no reason not to work.

"I have something for you," Philip called to say. Julia said fine but didn't fix her hair or change clothes, drawstring pants and a jersey.

He arrived empty-handed. "It's a massage. No protests." He covered her mouth. She was clairvoyant, he said; the outfit was perfect. He was unrolling a pad, popping a Bach harpsichord concerto on the stereo. She was face down on the floor.

"Petrified wood," he laughed, fingertips playing over the base of her skull, her neck, back, legs. Indeed Julia felt all hard grain, indissoluble knots. As his fingers probed she yelped and started to rise.

"Patience. Bear with me," Philip said.

Flowing blood did tingle in unexpected far parts of her body. Philip cautiously gave weight to his hands, then lifted her from beneath, let fall. Julia had the image of a board, clapped to her back, being pried loose. Now Philip could knead her flesh. The circling strokes of his palms were erasing her form. Even the pressure released her further.

"I don't feel anything," she mumbled into the cotton. "I mean, I do"—she laughed—"but I'm disembodied." The music advanced and receded, lacy waves breaking on the beach. She was a bubble, zigzagging from spume into the pure air.

Julia became absorbed in the carpet before her eyes, its thickness, geometry, flagrant colors. She tumbled through the weave, the pile separating, closing over her. "It yields like water," Philip panted, "and the colors stain your skin." Their merging of thought Julia accepted as natural.

Philip rolled her over, kissing. Their stripping altered nothing. She might always have been naked. At Philip's touch nerves opened until she was entirely this fresh, ageless openness. Caresses were partaking and giving in the same movement.

"These are *your* hands," she exulted.

Julia was swimming powerfully from shore, cutting a straight line through the water. When they finished she floated in a million miles of ocean, one with the currents.

"Now we truly are bonded," Philip said.

Energy begets energy—Julia's credo. Editing the zoo newsletter, she also drafted press releases and mailings to fund the stalled sun bear enclosure. Days off she and Philip might decamp for an Anasazi ruin, Mexico, the Santa Fe Opera.

Swimming sixty laps a day had firmed her muscle—and toughened the cardiopulmonary system, the doctor commended, examining her. She had virtually quit smoking. In Philip's presence she wasn't tempted. Exercise suppressed the desire in four-hour blocks, one before, one during, two after. The surviving indulgences, over tea and at bedtime, didn't satisfy as before, the inhalation pinched, and often Julia skipped even these.

A slow, hot July morning, she daydreamed in the zoo's information kiosk. Until he was upon her she didn't recognize him—Philip, in floppy beach shirt patterned with exploding firecrackers, cantaloupe-sized knees protruding beneath green bermuda shorts.

She laughed uncontrollably. "Alaska. Gigantic vegetables that grow in two weeks." She clipped the price tag from his belt loop.

Together they cast fish food from a keeper's bucket, a privilege of the veteran docents.

"Nice motion," Philip said of their arms' lazy sweeping. Cattails nodded in a breeze skimming cool off the water. Clouds puffed by.

"I'm happy," Julia said.

Linda, who missed the large family left behind with a past marriage, adopted Julia. Accompanied by Linda, Tim dropped by as often as twice a week. Without complaint he replaced a leaky faucet washer and soldered a loose connection in the stereo. "Need anything from Target?" he said. "I'm right there." A haunter of swap meets, Linda brought ceramic owl salt-and-pepper shakers, a touching, unusable gift.

"What do you do," Julia asked Philip, "on those weekends when I don't see you?"

"My survivalist cadre holds its potlucks."

"O.K." Julia held up her hands. "No questions."

"You know what would be lovely?" Julia said. A joint dinner for Philip, Tim, and Linda.

Philip was noncommittal.

After a few days Julia mentioned the idea again.

"My interest is in you," Philip said.

"But they are me, Tim is."

"That's an overpopulated armful for me." Philip smiled.

"Don't put me in a position where I have to have all these little drawers, 'Tim,' 'Philip' . . . Please."

"I like my drawer."

Though she hadn't disbelieved him, the tangible evidence of

Philip's literary accomplishments stunned Julia. She turned over in her hands the hard-paper quarterlies with their austere cover designs, to read his name on the contributors' lists. The most recent was ten years old.

She borrowed them. Rhymed but metrically unpredictable, his poems, even the youngest, were predominantly elegaic. One conjured a circus from its abandoned grounds, overgrown with thorns. In another two friends discoursed ironically on love amid the fleshpile of a public beach.

Always a reader, Julia now studied literature systematically, analyzing texts in a notebook, to prepare for talks with Philip. For his birthday she composed a poem.

"Poetry isn't your forte," he said, adding hurriedly, "but you are definitely in this poem. The sentiment is quite affecting."

When a rancher friend presented her with veal steaks, Julia again proposed the family dinner.

"Our balance is delicate," Philip said. "Let's not tip it."

"I wasn't aware," she said. "I thought we were quite robust. Tim and Linda keep asking to meet you."

Philip was adamant. "You haven't made Tim sound like the greatest company."

"How can you care for me and not want to know him?" Tightening vocal chords made Julia's voice strident. "You can't squirm away from them indefinitely. It's absurd."

"Why not? I'll credit them with going cheerfully about their business, content without stalking me."

Citing a need for "heart gossip," Linda brought lunch. So eager was she that Julia confessed, yes, she and Philip were "intimate."

"All right!" Linda pumped her fist.

Frankly, Julia said, the intervals between dinners were lengthening. Weekends, especially, were canceled. "A person doesn't

need sex. For nine years I did without. I didn't join a nunnery
or the Communist Party. I wasn't bulemic. Flying penises didn't
flock the skies."

Linda rolled onto her back, feet kicking. "You didn't grow a
beard. You didn't put ice cubes in your undies."

"How come I feel like I'm going nuts?" She'd awaken fighting
to breathe, as if steel bound her chest. The cough, when it came,
was a relief.

"I never know when Tim's going to show up either, two days,
a week, three in the morning."

"How do you stand it?"

"Here's me," Linda said, semicrouching. "I can go this way,
that." She pivoted left, right. "I never see Tim again, I'm sad, I'll
live. Meanwhile I have a helluva lot of fun. Take it day by day.
Tim zips me off to a ballgame, or picnicking in the mountains.
One night we made masks and grass skirts from newspaper and
called the house 'Hawaiian Zone.' And then . . ." Linda whistled,
drumming her fingers.

"Good for you. I don't see that side of Tim."

"I should hope not." Linda laughed.

"My idea of heaven," Julia said, "is two people giving recklessly
to each other, world without end. Amen."

"Why do I always initiate our lovemaking now?" Julia asked
Philip.

"You're the one who holds back sometimes. So I let you
choose."

"Don't you think maybe I'd like to be compelled by you, for
that to make my choice?"

"I'm not much for coercion."

"It's persuasion I'm asking for," Julia said. "I don't want it to
be all the same to you whether I say yes or no."

Philip prepared an evening of tantra, "a true yoga, serenity in
motionless sexual union." He positioned himself on the mat, the

half lotus. Setting Julia on his lap, hooking her feet around his back, he entered her. Within minutes his breathing had subsided to a dilation of the nostrils, sigh. His eyes shut, the blue-veined lids unclenching. The forehead smoothed.

Julia's skin burst with excitement and frustration. When finally he stirred, she choked her limbs around him, mauled his chest with her teeth. Quick-quick-quick she moved, bouncing her rear on his ankles, beating against him.

"I have to beg off tonight," Philip said over the phone. "My feet won't get me down the stairs." He'd been complaining.

Julia covered the hot dishes in foil and drove them over. "This place may have had its day," she said. "If you were closer at hand, I'd be more available."

"Is that a suggestion that I move in?"

"I suppose it is. The shambles is charming"—she gestured around the apartment—"but why not live graciously for a change?"

"Can you imagine us rattling around each other twenty-four hours a day?"

"It's not so outlandish," Julia said. She'd keep the top floor, he'd have the bottom, more territory than he was used to.

"Julia, your forays tire me."

"Me, too, Philip, I couldn't agree with you more. Please do me the one favor. Meet Tim."

A day later Philip said, "A concession on my part is called for. I'll come."

Philip was due at six. Tim and Linda arrived an hour early to help set up. Linda, diminutively voluptuous in a tight sheath, hair coiled, arranged the snack tray. Acting out family stories, she revealed a flair for mimicry. Tim had prepped for the evening to the extent of dredging up college lit notes. He discoursed on symbolism in *The Mill on the Floss*. Dusting the London broil with garlic, he quoted verbatim passages from *Anna Karenina* in the dog's point of view.

"Sweetheart," Julia said. "I'm really moved by this support." Tim kissed her.

A glass of sherry, intended to calm, made them giddier. Picking at the hors d'oeuvres, they had nearly emptied the tray when, at six sharp, the phone rang.

"I'm sorry, it's wrong. I feel coerced. We need to talk," Philip said.

Julia turned to Linda and Tim. "You guessed it."

"*Shit*," Tim said. The explosive "t" made the word particularly ugly.

Julia and Philip stood at his kitchen counter half an hour, as if sitting hadn't occurred to them. They conversed with a distracted fluency, statements already thought through that they now borrowed from themselves. Neither referred to a purpose for the meeting.

Julia asked why Philip no longer wrote.

He did, but rarely, nothing to keep. "I won't write depressed," he said. "That's ego, not poetry. I have no affinity with the vogue of inflicting one's every hidden recess upon 80 million readers."

Why so depressed? "Your feet," she joked.

"Yes." He laughed. "And my wife."

"Your ex-wife."

"I've resumed with her."

Julia rejected the attempt to believe she had mis-heard.

Vera was fifty, Philip said, still beautiful, copper hair and cream skin.

"Where do you go?" Julia asked numbly, as if interviewing.

"Here in town. Unfortunately, she's hopelessly unstable." After leaving him, Vera had jumped off a bandshell roof during a rock concert. "I moved her back in the house, and I left. I knew she'd be more at peace there."

Driving home Julia awaited the inevitable cough. Like the

braying of an onager, it came, accompanied by runny nose. She screamed in the closet, muffled by coats.

By phone she broke off with Philip. "I can't think of words to despise you enough," she said.

To expand the newsletter Julia recruited correspondents. The sun bear drive cracked its goal, and construction began. Member of a YWCA with indoor pool since fall set in, she slogged through laps when the cough allowed. Sunglasses hid the dark circles around her eyes.

The following weeks Tim was so peevish and erratic—most often Julia entertained Linda alone—that Julia considered imposing a once-a-month quota on *him*. Despite the persistent cough she again bought cigarettes. Linda berated her.

"At a certain age, character becomes simplified," she told Linda. "Julia plus Philip equals Tim minus smoking. Julia minus Philip equals smoking minus Tim."

Bundled in a quilt against the damp chill, feet to the electric heater, Julia thought of Easter, herself in the ambulance, a gray stick, tassel of brownish hair, the oxygen mask a malignant flower covering her face. The cough boomed.

Napping, Julia dreamed of Philip in the form of a joke. The prototype she'd actually heard, a series of exchanges, increasingly damning accusations culminating in a punch line that was, as usual, all she could remember. In the dream the words were enormous stone monuments, unreadable from her perspective. Among the letters Philip scurried, a gnome with hairy rump and tail, mischievously peeking. Some of the joke's lines, rather than words, were film clips of him—striding naked, leaning back from the table wiping his beard, among trees, tinted green from their leaves.

At the punch line—"Well, nobody's perfect"—Julia awoke laughing.

Through the church grapevine Julia learned that foot surgery had confined Philip to his apartment, his wheelchair unable to navigate the stairs. She assembled a CARE package of deli items, fresh fruit, and a bottle of Dry Sack, along with mundane necessities.

Grinning, Philip held out his arms. Even seated he was huge. "I've missed you so much," Julia said.

"Moscarpone! Smoked oysters!" He twisted the sherry cork and poured two glasses.

Lit only by a gap in the venetian blinds, the disheveled room showed no sign of outside intervention—a wife's, for instance.

Philip's bandages were cloddy white blocks. "The idea of someone cutting," he said. The wince bared his teeth. "I keep imagining them stepping into an egg slicer." For another two months he mustn't walk.

Julia did some picking up. "Today's man on wheels needs room to roll," she said, shoving books against the walls.

Philip beamed, sipping. "You are dear," he said. "Now we have a dance floor." He put on Vivaldi. Grasping Julia's hands, he lilted her to and fro. From behind, she lumbered him through figure eights. A hub caught books, loosing an avalanche. Deliberately Philip rammed another tower, toppling books and a broom, spilling the wastebasket. Flouncing her onto his lap with a thick arm, he said, "Have you ever made boom-boom with a mechanical centaur?"

"Philip," she said, "I love you, but that aspect of our relationship is past."

"My regret." Stretching for their glasses, he clinked. "And deepest apology."

Leaving, Julia demanded a key, and they argued. "What if you called for help and couldn't get to the door?" she said.

"All right." He slapped the key on the counter. "Not because I need it, but because you deserve it."

"Thank you thank you." Julia curtseyed. "I shall wear it like a diadem on my forehead."

"I'm an ass," Philip said. "Please take the key."

The morning of Christmas Eve, a dressed goose under her arm, Julia unlocked Philip's apartment and stepped into a glow like played-out neon, candles in red glass chimneys. "Boo," said the black hulk in the corner. "Happy Halloween."

Julia set the bird in the refrigerator and poured herself wine. "I apologize," Philip said. "I'm undergoing a seizure of reminiscence."

"You can talk about Vera," Julia said.

As if continuing an interrupted monologue, Philip said, "We were trekking in Nepal, our honeymoon. The sun fell toward the peaks"—his head dropped to one side and his voice thinned— "which went molten orange, as if just pulled from the fire by the glazier's tongs. Then we were rising, forced apart, until we found ourselves on separate peaks. The burnished ice fell away in all directions. We regarded each other across great distance, yet in perfect awareness and sympathy."

Philip's hands pressed together. "I steered our lives by that vision for years. So what if we were miserably incompatible. I willed us a couple, and now she can't live without me."

"I married my husband for his sadness," Julia said. "A mistake I undid. You're not bound to this lunatic!" she exclaimed.

"I become loquacious," Philip said, toneless. "I'm imposing on you."

"No, Philip. Wrong. This is what people do. They talk to each other." Her arm wrapped around his head, fingers in his beard.

Philip jerked back. "Ah, yes, the orgy of 'sharing':

'I have cancer of the bowels, and your breath stinks.'
'Thank you for sharing that with me.'"

"Call me when you are yourself," Julia said and ran out the door.

From a pay phone she retracted "lunatic." Until ambulatory, Philip said, he was unfit for company. They should limit contact to the telephone.

Obsessively Julia pictured Vera, red hair billowing, filmy dress clinging to her white limbs, bouncing on the pavement. Appalled at herself, she researched outings for Vera—chamber music, gallery openings, the botanical gardens, a bird sanctuary an hour's drive away. Reporting these to Philip, she added recommendations for therapeutic books and magazine articles.

"How is Vera today?" she asked him.

"Buzzing off the wall."

In this proxy existence, through Vera, Julia felt disconnected, as if there were no footing beneath her.

"Julia," Philip said, "our material is stale. My topics are few." He would be responsible for calls, which stabilized at two a week. Tacitly the phone arrangement remained in force even after his first gingerly steps, on crutches.

Linda commiserated over the passing of Julia's sex life.

"It's not even the sex," Julia said. "When he calls, I feel the same as when we used to make love. When he doesn't, it's just as maddening. Suffocating." In fact, she was resorting to a Bronch-Aid inhaler frequently for shortness of breath. Coughing fits had ended the swims. Mornings, swinging her legs out of bed, she'd fall back, dizzy. Her limbs always were cold, her legs felt leaden, two minutes' walk tired them.

The inability to smoke enraged Julia. To outwit her lungs she puffed while limp in a hot bath, or nearly asleep, over bourbon or steaming tea. Her lungs convulsed.

"I'm glad to see you and Linda working out," Julia said.

"I'm in a holding pattern," Tim said. "Eventually we'll break up."

"You were a sweet boy, Tim. There, I'm Generic Mom. But it's true. I have every card you hand-made for me, birthday, Mother's Day, Christmas, Easter, Valentine's, for twelve years. Our first visit to the Grand Canyon," she said, "we stepped to the edge, and the ground was broken in pieces as far as we could see. We grabbed hands, clasping so tight I think we both believed we could have floated down together. "And you know what? That boy still exists, as much as you do."

"You mean in your head. These guys are thirty-one." Tim wiggled his fingers.

She'd depended on him for a sense of future, Julia thought, not happy, simply tangible. But he defeated her like a TV after sign-off, a gray static buzz.

Philip sent a letter. "Our phone calls have outlived their usefulness. Increasingly they are an obligation."

Julia laughed out loud at herself, pacing the floor until she gained the equanimity to sit and type:

> You will be happy to read that this letter relieves you of your duties. Please don't call. Don't write. The books I've lent you, you may keep. Their meaning to me henceforth would be deformed.
>
> You probably consider withholding yourself as manly, a guarding of old virtues. It is not. It is monstrous selfishness. Caring people share themselves. I feel sorry for you. The loss is to us both.
>
> For the record, those burdensome phone calls, as our entire association, were delightfully stimulating to me.

Philip wore a loose gray shirt outside his pants, loafers sans socks. "Come in." He beckoned like a hotelier. The room was unchanged, though brighter, blinds open.

Julia handed him the envelope, which he laid on the counter. "Don't put it aside. Read it."

"Not under this scrutiny."

Julia slit the envelope with her fingernail and read the letter aloud.

Philip rubbed his face. "Quite fair," he said. "Points well taken." Off to the house, he said, for a packet of old manuscripts.

Come with? He hadn't invited Julia to his home before.

"Will she be there?"

"No. At the shrink."

Driving, Philip was expansive, head dipping toward her, hand flashing. In fantasy Julia had made this journey repeatedly— rescuing Vera from another suicide attempt, supporting Philip across the threshold after her death, tipsily dousing him with champagne after Vera's divorce. That she was actually round- ing Philip's corner she attributed to two factors. One, without a more satisfying resolution, which she would not get, she could not give up this final moment. Two, in Philip's view she no longer existed.

Tidiness shielded the interior of the solid brick house. Amazed at her detached curiosity, Julia searched for clues, nothing so obvious as a photo presenting itself. A pleasant scent, spicy, lin- gered. Philip rummaged in another room, drawers slamming. By the open French doors a curtain stirred.

Julia stepped into a profusion of snapdragons, tiger lilies, gladiolus, trillium, red poppies, crocus, plants she hadn't seen growing in the Southwest. Rustling trees filtered the sunlight. Cool, broad leaves slapped her thighs as each tread crunched, releasing a musky vegetable smell.

"I haven't trimmed the fruit trees. They're looking shaggy," Philip said. "I've wanted to introduce dogwood—those starburst blossoms are a vivid growing-up memory—but I suspect the cli- mate would be too much of a shock." He lowered himself, knees swaying, to pull a weed. "Planting the rose bushes was hell on my hands. My gloves weren't thick enough. Beyond punctures. Lacerations."

He looked up at Julia. "I retreated here from our love affair. This suits me. Vera and I scarcely meet. She's content to know I'm puttering nearby."

Julia saw the scene as a paperweight, an exquisitely-wrought foliation of colors, encased in glass. In the midst stood Philip,

feet transfixed by long pins topped with red hair. Placidly he
stooped with the watering can. It was set in Julia's mind, the
vision of what he'd chosen over her.

Although lying still in bed, curled on one side, Julia felt as
if she were bounding. Flinging out her limbs brought no relief.
She wrenched from side to side.

She dreamed she was floating on a sea of burning oil, the
ship's prow silhouetted, sinking. Fire crawled over her skin.
Thirst cracked her mouth. Flaming vapor wriggled skyward,
sucking oxygen, as the hot air collapsed, closed like a fist. Inhal-
ing, her lungs seared. Gasping, the sheets drenched, she yanked
the chain to the bedside lamp. The room's white and greens
harmonized tranquilly to the point of eeriness; the scene looked
stilted. Julia read.

A canopy of flame crinkled overhead, following her. Julia
would sit, hand to her chest, laboring for air. After a few yards'
walk her knees buckled.

Without loving Philip, Julia thought, she had sickened.
Loving him, she had sickened worse, more quickly. How could
it have become so simple?

Rising from the typewriter, the newsletter complete, she lost
her balance. She could not control her legs, which skidded
from under her. The second fall she waited until sensation returned, rubbing her calves. Crawling, she backed downstairs to
the phone.

Within minutes Tim was carrying her to the car. "Oh, no,"
he said, shutting the door, but the sound, broken as the latch
clicked, had no origin. It could have been spoken by the dashboard.

Tim whizzed through red lights, emergency flashers blinking,
horn beeping. His face was serene with purpose. Traffic in the
left-turn lane slowed them. Alongside, in the center median, a

cloud of butterflies bobbed across shrubs, an entity not quite whole, not quite dispersed. They reminded Julia of a meadow she'd once hiked years before, as a teenager. Breaking from the woods, she'd happened on a field strewn with deliriously yellow flowers. The air was so clear she'd felt no barrier between herself and the sky, earth, the fluttering petals. Running, with cleansing, full-chested pants, she leaped into their midst.

HUALAPAI DREAD

I

The Hualapai village of Alav lies at my back. The rocky path is steep. As I mount the ridge crest, a bicyclist is laboring toward me, up the other side. Though exertion makes holes of her eyes and mouth, she's beautiful, black hair tossing, skin buttery with sweat. Her bare midriff is taut over skimpy purple shorts. In the town of Hualapais, not exactly fat but rounded, dressed in modest anonymity up to the neck, she's a cover girl, a star. Her tires hiss. Pebbles crunch. She passes, and I look over my shoulder at her thinclad rear squunching on the bicycle seat.

Grasses are flared white in the sunset. Beyond the cliff shearing off the ground to my right, a line of hills runs toward the Grand Canyon, a gash on the horizon, veiled in orange light. I'm walking to acclimate, get the lay of the land. As new district manager for Associated Investment Services, out of Flagstaff, I've inherited one client in Alav, my last stop on a swing through rural Arizona. Damaged in last year's stock market crash, the goods—IRA's, cash management funds, limited partnerships, flexible annuities—aren't moving well.

Earlier today, when I first arrived in Alav, two horsemen rode straight down the middle of the street, broad copper faces unreadable, hooves scooping explosions of dust. To these people I must seem the human incarnation of a cash management fund, animated like a zombie: moussed forelock, suavely creased gray suit, red tie emblazoned on my chest. The thought brings up a capering chuckle in my throat, startling me. I would rather not have laughed that way.

By the time I rejoin Alav's main road, twilight has knitted the overhanging cottonwoods together and pulled them low. The cyclist is poised beside my car, one leg braced against the ground, the other foot on the pedal.

"Dooley," she introduces herself, and tells me she's a metallurgy student at the University of Arizona, on leave because her mother is ill. Meanwhile she's fighting fires, working construction—laid block on the new kindergarten wing.

"I don't know how I'm talking to you," Dooley says. "I look so atrocious. At the university I maintain myself, but here I don't even bother with makeup. At least I've had the morale to keep biking, so I don't swell up like a pig." Unconsciously—I think— she skims her belly. "I've done two hundred miles in a day."

"You must get hungry," I say. We settle on Chinese food in Worthington (home of six AIS clients), forty-five miles away. I feel dwarfed by my good luck. This admirable person.

In Dooley's triplex I wait and wait while the shower gushes, followed by an even longer silence. Mottled zigzags break up the TV screen. Dooley's mother is blind. A calico dress envelopes not only her shrunken body but the chair, stretching over its frame. The old woman seems to be resting in the embrace of a larger skeleton. She mutters to herself, not English. I can enjoy situations like this, if I have to.

With her Ph.D., knocking down fifty-sixty grand, she'd be able to afford decent medical care for her mother, Dooley had told me. "Indian Health Service"—she'd grimaced.

An hour after she started, she is beside me in a filmy black pajama suit, lavender sash matching her lip gloss. The black hair is a teased mane, heavy-lidded eyes shadowed blue. Her stalking prance ripples the black gauze and makes her silver earrings fly.

She drapes a blanket around her mother, leaves steaming tea beside. Her hand falls into mine.

Rolling onto the highway, I pull out the Stolichnaya 750 from under the front seat. The liquid filling my throat, it's as if an I.V. has hooked Dooley to me, and common fluids are circulating between us. I know we will be easy together.

She slides beside me and gently pushes the bottle down. "I don't think of alcohol as a pleasure," she says.

"You haven't drunk with the right people."

"I don't drink at all."

"Sure, no one says you have to. I can respect that. Just two more." I knock back the first.

Dooley sinks lower in the seat, the settling of her weight spreading her thigh against mine.

Through dinner I order tropical cocktails.

"You don't get drunk," she says.

It's true. Drinking is an eyepiece screwed into my head, that shows a woman standing forth as she should be, freed of all the crap that obscures our best selves. Dooley, model-gorgeous, on the cutting edge of space metallurgy, studying zero-gravity alloys, junks all to tend her sick mother. She'll get down and grunt to build a school for kids. She throws her body on the line, fighting fires. When Dooley excuses herself to the ladies' room, her turbulent walk concentrates the energy around her, releases it slowly, like a sky filling the restaurant. I lean back, floating in it.

Dooley's gone so long I worry that she's ducked out a back door. I enlist my neighbor, a ruddy, wind-whipped girl with taut braids—tough, understated, and hardworking, I can tell, the best qualities the Southwest offers, and she knows it, by the way she returns my look—to check on her.

"Just brushing her teeth," the girl reports, with a teasing poke to my shoulder. "Flossing now."

"Food catches in the spacings between my molars," Dooley explains. "Pop is a dentist."

Flying along the thread of road in the cool dark, I do the rest of the Stoly.

"You have to understand," Dooley says. "Everyone around here is a drunk. My father subjected my mother, my sister, and myself to abuse."

That's sickening. I can't bring myself to ask how. Instead, a tangent speaks. "A drunken dentist. What balls."

"No, no, that's Pop," she laughs. "He's Mormon. He's white." Through the LDS-sponsored Placement Program, Dooley had grown up with a Mormon foster family for seven years. Summers she'd return to the rez. The dentist still helped with college expenses. "Dad was the drunk. He's deceased. He was half Chinese. See? I eat Chinese and then brush my teeth."

I put my arm around Dooley and she leans close, breathing warmly on my hand. Drunkenness, like a big pat on the back, is sprawling me forward. My fingers play with the powerful features of Dooley's face, knobs and planes. I want to twist them off and keep them, but leave the face intact.

The motel where I'm staying is ten miles out of town. As I shut the car door, darkness billows around us. Dooley vanishes, replaced by a velvet intimacy. I pull her to me. Her tongue is fat and abandoned in my mouth. I caress her entire body, between her legs. "Go inside," I'm mouthing.

"I am not prepared for sexual intercourse," Dooley says.

O.K. Controlling my breath, I nod. Mormon thing?

"I can't remember when a man touched me as freely as you just did."

One habit I don't have is flattering myself. I can sense right away she has no use for the men in this town—no one's fault, incompatible backgrounds. And then there's the mumbling old lady with the awful slack eyes. A woman in these circumstances could fall for Son of Sam if he came from somewhere else and was going back there.

Meanwhile, we're inside. I'm pulling the light cord over the kitchenette, the cupboards that welcoming yellow of stained pine, and it's as if we're married, coming in off a long day's haul on the road, but it's vacation and every motel is our new home. Dooley and I stand under the light, kissing tenderly.

It seems I must have traveled cross-country with my family, cozying down in cheap, clean motels like this one, with tufted spreads and bars of light that rumbled across the walls with passing trucks. And I'm confused. I don't know if I'm the child whose shoes are about to be shaken into the wastebasket or if it's my own children I'm steadying on the bed as I loosen their snaps, roll down their socks.

But my mom cut out when I was five, and my dad ran an office machine repair year-round, so we didn't take trips, and I've never married.

Dooley surprises me, stripping completely for bed. Jackknifing, she whisks off her underpants, lean, muscular body bent like a hunting bow, the only softness her shuddering breasts.

She has these nervous caresses, as if she's straightening seat covers on her way out of the house. By now I'm on the faded side of the drunk, feeling like a cardboard cutout alone in a gray room. "So why the hell don't we just fuck?" I say, and she buzzes on about an eleven-month marriage, a white undergrad, sanctity of the marriage bed. "Pop is very strong in the Church," she says. She tells me, "My husband despised me because I am a nonwhite." I'm set in cardboard and her hand just rasps.

Morning I'm parched and rank, tremors jiggling my hands and feet. Dooley rubs me down.

We don't dress for breakfast, or all day. The drawn curtains keep a perpetual twilight. I'm aware that Dooley is offering her nakedness as a gift, her walk studied, experimentally nonchalant, her eyes flitting to the mirror. Opening the refrigerator, she poses prettily, hand on hip. Playing cards she squats on the bed, thighs spread wide.

The presence of her flesh draws my hangover like a salve. We talk, look out the window, deal gin rummy, eat, lie down. It's a normal day. Politely we maneuver around each other. I stroke Dooley's body appreciatively in passing, and she smiles.

At 6 P.M. I have an appointment with AIS's sole client in Alav, the elementary school principal. Chukka-chuk reggae guitar rings through the aluminum walls of her doublewide. Answering the door, the principal could be a softball coach with her long, untended hair and sateen windbreaker, except for the Stratocaster slung across her neck. Motioning me to the couch, she steps behind the mike. Dreadlocked portraits glower from the walls, one in lion headdress, spearpoint at his shoulder, another clay-yellow with a weird fringe of blond hair.

Bass and drums kick off. The principal sings, "I hear the words of the Rasta Man say Babylon you throne gone down, gone down . . ."

The band is Hualapai Dread, though only the principal is Hualapai, and no one wears dreadlocks. The rhythm section is Havasupai, while the plump white woman crouched over the synthesizer teaches kindergarten. Practice over, the principal joins me on the couch.

A Vegas dealer once told me his cards are a meditation, that while shuffling and distributing them he achieves the tranquility to make life decisions, including his vasectomy and conversion to Judaism. Laying out the AIS prospectuses, I feel solid ground beneath me. AIS is a well-marked path, with a handrail, and nearly drinking away this job a year ago was the worst hurt I've done myself.

Drinking really heavy, I was in command of the big picture, but details at the edges were eroding. Clients could have had legitimate issues with me. October 17, the market's Black Monday, obliterated those details, wiping my record clean. Since then, the extra time and effort I've devoted to clients—secretly I've even paid their custodial fees myself—is probably what got me promoted.

The principal's accounts are off 25 percent since the crash. She wants to build a recording studio. "Cut our own demo, sure, but for all musicians on the rez. You should hear the Hualapai Elvis."

Imaging the client in his or her ideal outcome directs me to the proper options. I see the principal in headphones, twirling knobs and slamming levers, torso pumping subtly to the beat. For rapid capital formation, I propose transferring the remains of her NewTech Fund into Precious Metals.

"Two-point-six percent in South African gold," she says, thumbing through the prospectus.

"Down from five-point-one. AIS is in the process of divestiture."

"None of that apartheid gold."

While admiring her principles, I can't allow her to abandon her goals. "You might consider," I say, "whether a symbol, with negligible real impact, is worth jeopardizing what you can accomplish here. Precious Metals is the portfolio's most aggressive performer. Forty-seven percent last year."

"Take it easy, King Midas." The band laughs. "Hualapai Dread doesn't make its music on the bodies of our African brothers and sisters."

"O.K. Good," I say.

I leave incredulous. Her investments will fail.

Without a couple of drinks I don't drop off at night. Dooley and I drive to a bar off the rez, where I wait in line at the package goods window. On the way back we hold hands, Dooley's fingers slipping in and out between mine, every so often a convulsive squeeze, our palms bellying against each other. I stop and we rub our faces together in just the same way.

Side by side under the covers, in the dark, we bring each other off. Our hands are slow, careful, and we never face each other.

"Friends would do that, for relief," Dooley says.

Drifting, I remember to ask after her mother.

"I've taught mother self-caring skills," Dooley explains. Through the monotone, stilted phrasing I hear clearly, Mother, release me, somebody get me out of this. Funny. Dooley's nudity is a mask, but the dense, crunched speech—her "deceased" father "subjecting me to abuse," "my husband despised me because I am a nonwhite"—is transparent, exposing her completely. I'm embarrassed and touched by these glimpses, as if I've peeped through a keyhole to see a woman not undressing, but weeping.

Wednesday morning we're heating water, stirring coffee, bumping, "excuse me." I slough about, genitals dangling irrelevantly, while Dooley tiptoes, spins, slings her hips, stretches over me to reach a light. Her nakedness chafes me like a shirt worn three days running. No matter how elaborate her excuses, the fact is she won't take me. I won't be able to please her.

I feel a horrible dwindling at this. My complicity in our arrangement makes us both a little repulsive to me. I'm in danger of being a freak. I can't see what more we have to do with each other.

"I've got business," I begin. "Your mother needs company."

Tears instantly fill Dooley's eyes. "Anyone would appear unattractive under the scrutiny you've given me," she says. "If you look at anything long enough, it becomes ugly. Try your own finger." Gripped in her fist, it almost touches my nose. "What is it?" she asks. "An intestine? A bone?"

Stunned at how deeply I've wounded her, I hold her tightly.

I say, "You've got it wrong." I propose a drive into the Canyon; pick her up at noon. Then, striding hard, I set out for the elementary school, trying to walk off the edgy boredom that's set into me.

I do need to schedule an AIS presentation for the elementary school faculty and staff. With 65 percent unemployment in Alav, they are virtually the only salaried inhabitants available. I find the principal surveying recess on the playground, arms folded. She greets me by humming "Goldfinger," resonantly. My Precious Metals defeat apparently has made me her pet.

Allotting me fifteen minutes during an employee picnic, after school tomorrow, the principal warns me that the gathering may be strange. The community is in mourning over the death of a great elder, a woman ninety-three years old. The tribe's last traditional healer and storyteller, she had found no one to take her place. For the first time in centuries, no living person will carry on this knowledge.

Head outthrust, knees pumping, Dooley bikes past the cyclone fence.

The principal orders me to tour the school with her. Classrooms are throbbing but orderly. The resource library displays thirty bilingual texts she co-authored with the dead elder. "What remains of her wisdom is preserved here." A history cover depicts the creation of the Hualapais from a reed in the Colorado. There's even an Eden story, the ancestral home of Madwida Canyon, where perennial springs watered farms of squash and beans. White settlers, the principal says, didn't credit the Hualapais with agriculture, and considered that proof of their low state. Having researched my clientele, I know that during the past century the tribe was almost exterminated by war, forced relocation, disease, starvation—a horrific downside and potentially divisive topic. Rather than turn the page, I ask the principal to read a line.

Though the words look like the sounds of choking, her voice gurgles and swishes, water flowing over stones.

I ask what she said.

"Your chin is big for your face." Laughing harshly, she tosses her head, peers sidelong to show it's a joke.

From the school parking lot I see Dooley inching up a rocky hill, standing straight on the pedals, wrenching the handlebars.

When I leave the market with tonic mixer, she's silhouetted on a ridgetop half a mile away, two wheels streaming hair.

Dooley enters the car leg first, denim mini slit up the hip, white boots matching her vest, makeup to the roots of her hair. Slouched in cutoffs, I soak in a thermos of gin and tonic. The car noses between yellow rock turrets, the sky a hammered blue. As we descend, the geology grows more ancient. Canyons multiply, coiling into the distance, somewhere the strongholds where Hualapai bands fled the soldiers, farther Madwida, ahead the Grand Canyon, now hidden by red sandstone walls.

All has converged to form the person beside me. Buoyant with renewed desire, I let her scent merge with the dry heat of rock. She's larger than myth. I could reach over and squeeze her breast, and she'd smile at me.

The washboard road drums steadily. Space opens and closes as canyons engulf us in shadow, recede.

The road is now a streambed, our tires splashing through puddles, grinding over boulders. Vivid greenery and driftwood stacks line the banks, the riparian dankness thickening. A presence in my ears has evolved into continuous booming.

There's the gorge. Blackened, twisted at the base, the wall rises through slates and browns to the red of viscera. At first it's hard to credit this muddy, churning little river with all the special effects. But it's very swift. Tracking its flow past a rock spur spins me dizzily.

Four yellow rafts have beached on the bank, a hub for scurrying white people, men and women bare to the waist, wiry, sand-caked, with dried-bush hair. Incredibly, I recognize college classmates, a racquetball partner, my insurance agent and her husband; it's a Flagstaff expedition. I introduce Dooley, who nods absently, wandering off among piles of gear and Hefty bags swollen with beer cans.

Making small talk with my topless State Farm rep is a heady experience. The bubbling gin and tonic leaves an herbal wake. Where a channel loop has stalled into a backwater, rafters are skinnydipping. Dooley looks neither left nor right, white vinyl ledges of her shoulders tipping as her high-heeled boots pick deliberately through loose stones. Unbooting, she stands in the shallows, arms straight at her sides, eyes closed. I imagine her striding into the river, body russet like the canyon reflected on the water, a piece of that reflection upright and walking. I anticipate the lull in activity, hush, as we immerse ourselves together.

The beauty of that moment will redeem what has gone on between us.

"Come on." Beside her, I drop my cutoffs.

Her face gapes. "I share myself only with you."

"The river will cover us." My whole self is forced into the narrow crooning of my voice, so convinced I am, the water around us like a skin.

"The tribe strictly prohibits—"

Though I intend the tug on her buckle to coax, the belt jumps free with an audible crack.

Folding her clothing, Dooley wades naked through the eddies, launches herself in a slow stroke. Her face has gone inward, she looks asleep, hair fanning on the murky water, her form undulating beneath the surface. Revolving with the current, she circles the swimmers. I try to intercept her hand, but she springs onto the bank, shimmering, goosefleshed. A group is drip-drying, whipping their hair and stamping their feet. Dooley accepts a beer! Gesturing airily, she chats, scratches her leg. Her pebbly nipples are stiff. The boatman jokes and she rocks back, laughing, fingertips at her breastbone, then lightly pushes his arm.

"So why didn't you just shake your pussy in his face?" I say. We're jouncing over the streambed, steering wheel fighting my hands. The image of my Dooley—since when did she become my Dooley?—stripped and at ease, body playing to the boatman's voice, reruns and reruns.

"I was clothed," she says. "In my mind I dressed myself in your beautiful suit." Her hands grasp my arm. "I was hidden from my neck to my feet." She knots an imaginary tie. "I was so confident. I stood erect, moved my hands decisively, and I looked everyone in the eye like a white person."

I have a brainstorm: I will attend the wake and pay my respects to the dead elder. The opportunity for visibility in the community, networking, is not to be missed. And there's spite—the exclusion of Dooley, who I'm sure won't take part in the ritual.

"You don't belong there," she says. "I don't either. But you don't."

"So by logic we should go together."

Dooley shakes her head. Maybe at dawn, she says, for goodbye. That's when the spirit leaves the body.

Night is falling as we reach Alav. I peck Dooley's cheek and go to change.

The gymnasium is a looming old hulk. Inside, light, concentrated on the casket heaped with flowers, dissipates into a gloom of struts and the invisible ceiling. Rows of mourners in straight-backed metal folding chairs recede into darkness. A woman, gray hair wildly flying, rigid arms ending in fists, upbraids the gathering in a raw, tearful singsong.

The principal, balancing a paper plate, is eating solemnly. She glances up sharply, eyes reddened and blurry. "No briefcase?" she says. "I thought you came to sell her an IRA." Her head nods toward the bier.

"What's the woman saying?" I ask.

"It's the oldest daughter. 'You never heard my mother in your hearts when she was alive.'"

The speaker's lamentation cuts the air thrillingly. Flowing, colorful dresses are tacked across the front wall. The one in the center, behind the casket, is most noticeably empty.

"'She looked at us, the Hualapai, and saw what we have been. Who will see that now?'" the principal translates. Thumbing toward a window in the back wall, the principal says, "Eat."

The square of light is so radiant I can scarcely discern the kitchen help, whose bustling shapes are shifting densities of brilliance. I'm glimpsing the sphere of the blessed, long-departed ancestors, industrious, bountiful. Hands emerge from the glare, a floating face, offering a flat cake like a thick tortilla, beans.

I've stepped through a slot in the earth, into the underworld. The speaker's keening washes over me, like the river's echoes splintering off the gorge hours ago. Mourning. Suddenly the word catches my chest, fills my throat. It becomes Dooley standing shocked, beltless, in the water. It is our bodies exchanging stiff caresses in a dim motel.

I'm in a town at the edge of the world, whose inhabitants speak another language, trying to sell them devalued paper, which they reject. I'm sneaking handjobs and humiliating the girl who gives them to me—but she disappointed me! she didn't measure up!—but these thoughts are wrong, they are part of my grief.

This is all I know to do. I'm thirty-three and have no memories of anything. When I try to think of home, Flagstaff is no more than those companions of today, magnificently healthy animals scudding across rapids in yellow balloon-boats.

Nothing is the way I want it. I can't imagine how I would

want it. The sobs around me are too powerful to resist. My own throat is jumping. I concentrate on the paper plate of food.

A bald priest, the only other white, leads a women's chorus in a tremulous hymn. Another eulogist takes the floor. As new arrivals cluster, a group rises and, single file, shakes hands across the front row of mourners, then exits. With each departure, singly, in pairs or threes, entire rows, the handshaking is repeated. The openings and closings of doors stir the empty dresses.

The bereaved family, the principal explains. "When you leave, you do the same."

"But they don't know me from Adam."

"You don't ignore the family. That's a bad mistake. They've noticed you. You've got yourself in a spot, coming here. Go on over, give them your Midas touch. It'll be interesting to see what happens."

I'm honored to commiserate with them. As I approach from the aisle, the row of bowed heads is interminable, men, women, elders, children, crew cuts, braids, long bangs. Nearer, the heads are lustrous, redolent of shampooing. Holding out my hand, I see a startled upturned face. The handclasp is inert, one hand laid within the other, without the vigorous pumping I'm used to, strangely intimate. Though a few faces look frankly into mine, most remain lowered. Some hands, then more and more, are reluctant to take mine. By the end, the hands stay in their laps. Flushing, extended palm sweating, I pass blank faces.

Thud of the door behind me, out in the cool air I'm aware something irrevocable has happened. I'm in the car, kicking the gas, headlights cleaning the highway, when it hits me. This gig is over, I'm through.

I must have driven an hour or more when I pull off at a saloon full of Hualapais, whom I avoid, opting for the cowboys at the bar. ESPN is rehashing World Series game #4, the Dodgers going up 3 to 1 over the A's.

A Hualapai approaches, compact, slick-haired, unsteady on his boots. "Father, I need to talk to you," he says.

He's not focusing, hands outstretched in front of his chest, holding an emptiness the size of a beachball. I give Canseco's slow-motion strikeout my undivided attention.

The man has my forearm.

"Do I look like your father?"

"Don't jack me around, Father. Shit."

Shaking loose, I vault from the barstool.

"Father, I need to confess," he says. "I've done something terrible."

Down the street, the motel bar is bright and empty, upholstered in vinyl pastels, like a mausoleum by Denny's. I drink 'til closing.

Driving to Alav I take it easy. I don't want to hurt myself, I don't want to hurt anyone else. On the creaky porch chair by my motel room is a plate. Unwrapping the tinfoil, I see chocolate chip cookies, with a note, "Sorry I was so flippy today." I eat every delicious cookie, must contain two packs of chips. I lie down on the bed with those cookies in my stomach, but Dooley is in my head, circling in the Colorado, body glistening as it breaks the surface.

Rapping at Dooley's window, I hear a beeping, tiny, not a burglar alarm. I can't figure it out and almost run, but Dooley's face appears at the glass. In the doorway her flannel nightgown runs to the floor, her head and hands disembodied. TV glow illuminates her mother—World Series highlights at four, five in the morning. Video disturbance leaves the players' limbs suddenly, grotesquely distended, their uniforms' colors detached, smeared above them.

"I was just getting up for Rachel," Dooley says. Rachel is the dead elder.

Dooley's room is geometrically neat save for the ruffle of turned-down bedsheet. "I didn't think I was going to see you," she says, looking away. I guess we talk about the wake—I hear our murmuring. Unlacing the bodice, she draws my face to her breasts, fingers in my hair. My hands at her hips gather folds of nightgown, reeling it in until I touch bare skin. Cupping her buttocks, I kiss her breasts, warm neck. So we can be closer I unfasten my pants, let them fall, prod against her.

She straight-arms me, staggering us both backwards. "No. I can't have sex with you."

Then I'm lying across her chest, on the bed, hand clamped over her mouth, an irrelevant, intrusive hand, black-haired, knobby bones sticking out at the wrist. My legs sprawl wider, my left hooks her right. I'm trying to align myself over her while she struggles marvelously, legs whipping—the strong, wonderful body that stoops, hoisting block, the muscles bunching and lengthening, a room where decades of children will learn—that same body pitted against fire, feet planted, arm muscles ropy, the hair falling against her blackened cheek.

I have the nightgown around her neck, but there's a strange noise, no, absence of noise. The TV is off. Footsteps clump through the house. I seize the mental picture of a withered, blind old woman lost in calico. But I see an empty dress waving, hear wailing bursts of speech, rags of the Hualapai tongue. It is dawn, when the spirit leaves the body. The dripping, decaying river odor invades the air. Dampness brushes my neck.

A shudder snaps my spine, and I let up. Dooley and I rise to sitting, as if inflated. Footsteps pause at the door. Dooley and her mother exchange words I don't understand. Another door closes.

I look at Dooley in agony. I can't dress quickly enough.

Confirming that the wake fiasco has canceled my presentation, the principal isn't unkind. "By next year we will have many other stupid blunders by white people to talk about, and you can try again. We'll say, 'Maybe he's the new, improved model now.'"

Her husband, the tribe's hydrologist, who has been in Phoenix testifying before the state Supreme Court, may be a prospect.

I can't see either tossing Dooley's cookie plate in the garbage or leaving it for the motel manager. She's not at the triplex, so I walk my first day's route, encountering her on the exact same ridge, or one identical to it. Braking, she wheels the bike several yards in from the cliff, digging in her feet. Sweat welds my underarms to the suit jacket.

Her entire face contracts into a frown when I offer the plate. "I don't want it. How am I supposed to carry it?"

I lay the plate at her doorstep on my way out of town.

II

A year later, Alav looks diminished. Where I remember scattered board houses sinking into the hillsides at dusk, while windows of the ridgetop subdivision boiled with reflected suns and shawled old women glided over the land like the shadows of birds, I see a doublewide advertising martial arts videos, burgers, and Dr. Pepper. A pod of satellite dishes is interspersed among the tract homes. Children dash between derelict backyard appliances, their shouts very much of this world.

The scene hasn't changed, of course, but my perceptions, no longer hyperbolic with alcohol.

I quit drinking soon after coming home to Flag. I'd begun seeing a girl, sixteen, very beautiful like Isabella Rossellini in *Blue Velvet,* and an accomplished pianist. But she was erratic returning my calls, and I never knew where I stood.

Failing to connect on a Saturday night, I went to the NAU game with friends. We shared flasks and had drinks after. I found myself outside the girl's house. The porch light was on, the interior dark. I let myself in and padded toward her room, shoes off, the floorboards groaning. I kept seeing a picture of her: seated at the piano, playing show tunes. The notes sprang from her head as black curls, roping, twining down her white back. Her buttocks rocked. The hair cascaded over her skin.

Her room was empty. I couldn't believe it. The red dial glowed 12:41. She always made her one o'clock curfew.

I went from room to room, the mother, the majestic, big-boned older sister, the little brother, who alone had the girl's black hair and white skin. They were coiled in sleep like Pompeiians. I touched each of their faces.

On our reconciliation date I told the girl what I'd done. She left the bar immediately. The loss was too vast to comprehend. It felt like I'd be swallowed up if I tried to take a step. I switched from vodka collins, our drink, to gimlets.

A woman who always took me would be just getting off the swing shift at the hospital lab. I bulled across the space between me and the lounge door and made the car. The woman was petite, neatly built, whimsical, but self-deprecatory. Her job was scrutinizing slides of infected tissue. The light of her one-room apartment was on. She'd be lying with her feet up in front of the TV. She would be glad to see me.

I sat on the fender. The November night was cold. Knocking on the woman's door seemed an act of utter disrespect. I tried to talk myself out of this attitude. Eventually I lay in the alley and slept until dawn. Waking, I was so grateful to myself that I cried.

Drinking had the coherence of a narrative, each drunk its beginning, middle, and end. Everything now is wisps, traces. I feel drained, as if my oversugared blood has been drawn and is hanging close by but out of reach, a red mist, rain that evaporates before touching ground.

On the computer I composed a basic letter of apology, which I've adapted for the various people I've harmed. This project alone took months. Some responded, which is gratifying. I enclosed a note with Dooley's copy. I sign the letters "love," but for

Dooley I intended more. "All my love" and "much love" seemed inflated and inadequate. So I just left my name. She hasn't replied.

The principal has assembled the potential AIS investors among faculty, aides, and staff at a Hualapai Dread rehearsal. This translates into an audience of four, myself the fifth.

"As you know," the principal says, "Hualapai Dread makes its off-rez debut this Thursday, at the Elks Club, Worthington, Arizona." The teachers whoop. "Be there and accrue district increment credit. Naah," she laughs. "We're going to do an original now."

The synthesizer lays down a riff. Flicking the guitar strings, the principal chants,

> Come Mandela
> They go a fire
> South Africa.

After a forty-five-minute set the audience cheers and stomps. The principal announces, "And now, ladies and gentlemen, we have a very special treat for you, a fine entertainment, a financial wizard telling you how to become rich like him."

The atmosphere not particularly conducive to comprehensive financial planning, my presentation arouses only mild interest. Heads pore over the glossy pages of tables and graphs while I circulate, answering and posing questions. The overall AIS rate of return has stabilized. It won't hurt anybody.

Vernon, the principal's hydrologist husband, is slightly taller than my five-eleven, with an iron gray crew cut and seamed forehead.

"King Midas Mufflers," he says straight-faced. We work out a few cautious investments as he talks up his wife, who has devised an entire bilingual curriculum through sixth grade. Fifteen years ago, he says, Hualapai had no written language. Now

80 percent of Alav Elementary's students graduate high school, 30 percent attending college.

"Don't tell me," the principal says, joining us. "Hualapai Dread is Fortune 500 now."

"Congratulations," I say. "You're almost breaking even, back to pre-1987. At this pace you'll have your studio in twenty-five years, max."

"Gives me something to live for." With Precious Metals clinging to .5 percent South African, she declines moving her funds.

"Dooley around?" I ask. "I went by her place today."

"Gone all week," the white keyboardist-kindergarten teacher yells over. "Her cousin is in a volleyball tournament at Tuba City."

"That is, if they don't lose," Vernon laughs. "She might be home tomorrow."

"Vernon, why do you want to make it easy for him?" the keyboardist says. "Sure, let him shack up with his Indian dolly again and then take off without a word until his next godlike visitation. Indian people are patient. Indian people will sit up on their hind legs for his scraps of affection. That woman wandered around like a ghost for weeks after he left."

Quiet.

"I treated her," I begin, shaking my head, ". . . inexcusably . . . there's no word." I'm glad to be saying this publicly.

"She makes everyone feel that way," the principal says. "When I pass her on the street, a little voice inside starts yelling 'apologize,' and I don't know for what."

Wanting to confess everything, I check myself in time, considering Dooley's privacy. Apparently she's told no one. Once again—the market crash, two years ago—I, that self I was, is jerked off the hook. I'm ashamed at my relief, helpless with it.

Aside, the principal says, "Is it true Dooley has 365 separate outfits?"

"I haven't gone through her wardrobe."

"You know she doesn't pay a dime on that place of her mother's."

But her jobs, the construction, firefighting.

"One week each, over a year ago," the principal says.

And yet she's brilliant, I say, preparing to enter an elite profession in, what, her mid-twenties?

"She'll love you for that. She's thirty-five." Still an undergrad, with brief stints at Eastern Montana, the University of New Mexico, and Arizona State before the University of Arizona.

My obligation to Dooley is simple: face to face, I ensure that she give up, to me, any blame she might feel for what happened. I do all I can to heal her, whatever she asks, and say good-bye. But leaving the doublewide, I find myself wanting to touch Dooley. It's the first desire of any kind in months. I think of my hand flat on her back, or our fingers linked, and my heart falls open.

She is at home Thursday, after I've killed two days. "So you're here," she says. I'd written ahead. Her hair shoots over a fluorescent headband, her bare shoulders look hard and smooth.

Arms tight at my sides, I invite her to the Hualapai Dread concert.

Her mouth suddenly twists. "I need a minute with God, to compose myself," she says. "Please excuse me."

The sun streams bright around my shadow in the open doorway. It's more like ten minutes.

"If I don't stare down fear," Dooley says, "it will never go away. God will sustain me."

When I pick her up, her mouth is orange. A stiff ponytail lies across one shoulder. The acid-washed mini is relatively demure. Opposite her mother, the World Series warm-up replays last year's clinching Dodger victory. Snowed under by the usual video interference, the fielders perform thickly. The camera zooms in for a close-up of Hershiser, baby face smiling seraphically, murderous right arm hidden behind his back. The Dodgers insignia crawls across his chest like a rebellious organ, or a trivial, visible portion of soul. Dread, the memory of a year ago, flexes in the pit of my stomach. I wait for it to subside.

I'm as jittery as Dooley. Desire blows at me and I duck away. Then it comes back. I want to squeeze Dooley to my chest and just hold her. I actually become dizzy. It's maddening. And still we manage small talk on the drive over. She likes reggae, she says. At the university she goes out dancing a lot, and she's friends with the trumpet player in a blues band. Her mother is "steady," she says.

On the outskirts of Worthington Dooley begins a morbid roll call at the passing bars. "That's Ronnie Sinyalla's green pickup. Henry Wescogame, Alvin Burt . . ." The cubicles leak the occasional neon beer emblem. Vehicles are stark under streetlights, or dim shapes like holes in the landscape. Dooley reels off more names. The bars encircle the town, reminding me simultaneously of a bivouacked army and of refugee camps. "Drunks," Dooley barks, and her fists strike her knees.

The Elks Club is concrete block, windowless. Seated on folding chairs, the crowd of sixty or seventy appears mostly Hualapai, with a few whites, Mexicans, and one black man in a wool cap red, green, and yellow. Though I recognize faces, no one acknowledges us. Dooley and I take the back row. Security guards, flashlights and sticks dangling by their holsters, line one wall.

Somebody has shelled out for new, big speakers. The principal steps up to the mike. "Welcome to the first stop on Hualapai Dread's world tour," she says. "We're going to do Bob Marley's 'Exodus.' Remember, our permit doesn't allow dancing." She wrinkles her face.

"Dance on your butts," the bass player calls.

The insistent power beat isn't typical of reggae. Dooley juts her shoulders, shimmies. The crowd rocks slowly, introspectively, heads down. Dooley's wrist bangles jingle. Her enjoyment makes me achingly fond of her, the more so because I've seen it so rarely. Even the fraud of her life becomes dear, an invention she's made, just as an artisan might fashion a vase, pinching the handles like *this* and elongating the neck like *this*.

But I'm straitjacketed. I can't put my arm around her, nudge my shoulder into hers. If our elbows touched, she'd jump.

By the third number, several young men are on the floor. The band disregards them. The principal sings the Mandela song. When the snaking bodies have filled the space between seats and the band, security moves in, surrounding the microphone.

"The authorities remind us that dancing is prohibited," says the principal. The dancers ignore her. A burly security guard snatches the mike. "Return to your seats immediately or this concert will be stopped." More rise and take the floor.

Abruptly the hall is blacked out, the music silenced except for the bashing drumbeat. Almost instantly the principal's voice penetrates: "Truly there is darkness in Babylon." But our laughter doesn't restore the power. Footsteps reverberate, flashlights pinpoint an individual face, then vacancy. Chairs crash and the side doors are thrust open. Streetlights reveal a knot of twenty or so in the aisle, swaying, strutting, arms pumping to the drum. Their intensity—eyes closed, mouths grimacing, heads nodding as if to push aside the air—frightens me as much as the security guards converging on them. The cymbals go over with a clang. Thuds, a long, rippling tinkle. Screaming. Grabbing each other by the arm, Dooley and I bolt outside.

The car's passenger window is smashed, so Dooley dives in my side. We fishtail down the alley as a train of police cruisers hops the curb, flashing lights sweeping the parking lot. Though I rig a seat cover over the hole, cold air whistles in. Dooley clasps her arms around her chest, huddling against the heater vent. She accepts my jacket.

"They couldn't arrest her, could they? How do they work around here?" I say.

"You saw how it works."

"Please come back with me. I never dreamed I'd say this. I never dared think I could say this."

"To your motel?"

I think that's what I meant, but the wrongness is obvious when the words come out of my mouth, and scrambling, improvising, with confused happiness I hear myself saying, "No, to Flagstaff. I'm not the same person, I swear. Who did what I did. That person is dead."

"God bless you," she says. "I'm very happy for you. But I am the same person."

Downshifting at Alav, my hand repeatedly bumps Dooley's bare thigh, an accident neither of us bothers to acknowledge. I don't linger; she doesn't move.

"How can I maintain an acquaintanceship with such a discourteous person?" Dooley says. "Hunting me down with your plate, then leaving it on my doorstep like a gob of spit."

It's a moment before I realize what she's talking about. "I didn't mean anything. I just didn't want to drive off like I owned it."

"You did own it. I gave it to you. A gift is not a decision. It's not a question. Someone gives you something." Now she's crying. In the darkness her eyebrows have vanished. Her eyes and teeth are pale. The grief-mask cuts deep furrows in her brow. At the triplex I touch her hair. "No, I'm done now," she says, and she's out.

As I lie in bed, near sleep, what Dooley told me unrolls like the murals you see in Arizona's old territorial banks. An armored man extends a gleaming, empty plate toward a dark woman, nearly nude, on her wheeled contrivance. His look is downcast. She scowls, tears running from her eyes. The bicycle wheels rotate over stony ground at the edge of a glorious abyss, voices echoing down a maze of painted corridors, emptying into the river.

You believe what you say, that you're not the same person.
You're starting clean, you've cut free from the drag of the past.
Everything is open to you. And then it turns out you're in history
all along, yours and everybody else's.

I'd like to think a time will come when this story between
Dooley and me seems so remote that I'll look back in disbelief.
But I expect I'll always see the sorrowful mask of her face as I
do now, floating just out of reach.

THE MARCH OF THE TOYS

Leah and I met at a refrigerator, a party thudding through the walls. She was flushed and perspiring. I wore a beige dress that screamed, if beige can scream, Don't look at me! I'm not really here!

I'd recently broken up with a man and was living ineptly, at cross-purposes. Why else attend a dance party, single, with no interest in a partner? I stand, I watch, I go home.

There was only one beer in the fridge.

"Go ahead," said Leah—though I didn't yet know her name. "I'll stick with tequila."

It shocked me, minutes later, to see her laughing out of control, teeth bared, eyes squinted shut. Ha ha ha ha ha, she laughed, a spooky bird sound. For months after, I disregarded the moment, as if I'd been mistaken. Leah and this person couldn't be the same.

Her boyfriend was arranging stick pretzels in another woman's cleavage. Then they left together, he and the pretzel woman. I looked out the window. A white pickup barged off.

I offered Leah a ride.

"I can't go home," she said. "What if he never shows up?"

Leah spent the night on my couch. In the morning I served us breakfast.

"This is like the tundra." Leah gestured around my barren apartment. Six weeks after leaving my lover I'd acquired only a Finnish dining set and a matching overstuffed rattan chair and couch.

Leah was fidgety, anxious to go. When I dropped her at home, the white pickup was in the drive, and she relaxed. Thanking me, she invited me back for dinner. Soothed by the role of spectator at someone else's drama, I said yes.

The man I'd left, large, balding, mat of hair on his chest, had reminded me of Gerald Ford. Star athlete, a handsome, friendly guy—I've never understood the derision heaped on President Ford. Instead of guiding the nation, though, my Jim took long walks and occasional carpentry jobs. As his money ran out, he drank hard liquor, aggravating his ulcer. Our last weeks, he was vomiting nightly. I would wake just before the sound began. After twice finding the toilet filled with blood, I would close my eyes and flush when I entered the bathroom.

My first impression at Leah's was that I'd entered a sunken living room. But, outside of two standing brass lamps, it was the furniture itself that was low, the long couches and tables. Cushions were strewn everywhere, collecting in mounds along the walls. Leah took a place among them, I beside her. Sitting, we were nearly reclining.

The pillows were boldly quilted, some resembling vegetables, clouds, mustaches. She made them to sell at street fairs, she said, and for steady income taught math at the JC. "Lies," she laughed. "All I do now is fuck."

"I take it such an event has occurred since this morning?"

"Why ye-es." Last night was a farce, she whispered. Eskison, the boyfriend, had taken the pretzel woman for cigarettes, and they were back ten minutes after we left. When Leah wasn't home, he'd called the party, but no one knew my address. "Idiot," Leah said, her forefinger making the "crazy" circle at her own head. "Sorry."

Yeah, but what about the pretzels in the décolletage?

" 'I couldn't let her get away with dressing like that,' " Leah quoted him sarcastically. She spread her hands. "He sucks."

Both she and Eskison, who now appeared from the kitchen, seemed light-headed with the reconciliation.

"The rescuer," he said, shaking my hand. "I should sue you for mental agony. I didn't sleep a second all night."

"I countersue you, on the same grounds," Leah said. They laughed uproariously. Eskison stiffened his body, arms rigid at his sides, eyes bulging—" 'What's she doing?' 'What's he doing?' "

Small and dark, curly hair and beard encircling his face, he was in his mid-twenties, I guessed, Leah approaching forty. I was twenty-five, and subtracting the glamor of youth, he wasn't so great.

After dinner, while Eskison smoked outside, Leah and I told stories about our neighbors, mine young singles, hers Mexican families established for generations. "You glazed over," she said. "Am I talking too much? Do you want coffee?"

Teaching myself moment to moment to live with my lover's absence occupied me so completely, only then had it occurred to me I was going home, to Delaware, the next week.

"Trouble?" Leah asked.

When I was ten, I explained, Lou Gehrig's disease, ALS, was diagnosed in my father, and he was given five years to live. Continuing to work a decade, he'd then sold his housepainting business. Fifteen years after the first symptoms, doctors were confounded by his protracted dying.

"That's awful," Leah said. Embarrassingly, I couldn't speak. My mind was blank. After a respectful silence, she added, "Stop by when you're back, if you need fixing up."

Then Eskison's truck started, and Leah's face sagged.

"Probably going for more beer," I said.

"*Es posible.*" Leah waved her hand dismissively. She sat on the couch, crossed her legs, fluffed her hair. Seeing that she was postponing a fit until I left, shortly I did.

The next morning she called to apologize for her "edginess." I was right about the beer. She wished me luck.

My brother Rick picked me up at Greater Wilmington Airport, in a '56 Thunderbird. Top down, we zoomed past slushy ice, Rick's hair blown back in a crest. Dark birthmark beneath his right eye, cigarette tip pale orange in the wind—dashing Rick.

Home, my mother scurried about the kitchen, her red face puckered and shiny as a baked apple. As usual, during our hug she looked away, as if worried that somewhere something was boiling over.

From the wrinkles across his shirt I knew that Dad had been lying down. He was so emaciated the skin and white mustache drooped from his face like the shirt from his frame. Wrapping my arms around him, I pressed his back.

Mother cut his meat at the dinner table. After dessert we watched TV in the den. On the seven-foot screen a quarterback threw his pass into the stands. Rick sat hunched, neck in a U, cracking his knuckles. "Got to thrash tonight," he said, standing.

"Rick!" Mother said. "You won't see Claire again until God knows when."

"We'll do tomorrow." Rick winked at me.

"Movie, hon?" Dad said.

"I like the game, Dad." We always watched together. I would sit in his lap, beside him as I got older, sharing sips of beer, breathing the turpentine that never scrubbed out.

By halftime Dad's jaw dropped and he stared as if aghast at the colored figures piling up on Astroturf. Mother and I stretched him on the hide-a-bed, drawing a comforter to his chin.

"When we bought the couch, nobody guessed how well it fit him," Mother said. "See? His feet go right down to the end."

Mother had grown so inward, I didn't always know how to respond.

Without Rick in the house I was lonely. We hadn't always been close. Until Dad's illness I barely acknowledged Rick, four years younger. I was the first, he was the boy. We each had our claim. What I do recall is the garden variety ruthlessness, I "forgetting" to remove the baby gate from the stairs, Rick left wailing as I played loudly below; an older Rick parading buddies through the bathroom while I showered.

When I first learned about Dad, I pushed in loose concrete blocks and crawled under the house. In the dark I dug elbows and heels into the cool earth. Footsteps above rained dust and cobwebs on me. I stuffed dirt in my mouth, cramming it down with my fists. A strand of web stuck to my lip. I couldn't detach it with tongue or fingers. I gagged, spitting. I screamed. They had to drag me out by the feet.

Gradually, as far as Rick was concerned, I took over for Dad. I walked Rick to tee-ball and then Little League practice, and watched. Sometimes they had me get in the pickle, not often, because I was too fast. The parental stand-in at Open House, I promised to ride Rick about his homework.

To finance Dad's cure we threw a paper route. I could see Rick pedaling furiously abreast of me, newspaper cocked behind his ear. His face, still pudgy, sweated, veins swelling.

Rick and I drove around. Since he insisted on keeping the top down, we were bundled like polar explorers. The sky was raw and leaden with clouds. We shouted through traffic noise and earmuffs. Rick approved that I'd broken up with Jim, whom I'd met the first month after I moved to Tucson three years before.

Rick and I had a tradition of confiding our most intimate

romantic details while the listener dissected the lover merci-
lessly.

"You undersold yourself on that Jim," he said. "After Vinnie
Toglia, you go out there and take up with an old bald bum."

"Vinnie Toglia was a sadist."

"You handled him. That Camaro was the most loaded thing
this side of NASA. He's got his own dog-grooming business
now." The other half of the tradition was that, once departed
suitably long, these maligned lovers took on wonderful attributes
and their loss was seen as a tragic error in judgment. Within
a year or two, I assumed, Rick would have canonized Jim—
"oddball, but he showed you respect, a gentleman."

"I was in a bad space when I was seeing Vinnie," I said. "I can't
stand this. My face is frostbitten."

"Arizona has wimped you out."

We fought a few blocks before Rick curbed the T-Bird and
attached the top.

"Rick," I said once we were moving, "what will you do when
Dad's gone?"

"Fuck knows. Jack around with cars, I guess, free-lance, a
garage."

Rick parked at a renovated corner market of graying brick,
the window veined with neon. I would treat him to this video
arcade on the way home from Little League.

"Ding-dongs, salted nut roll, and two cream sodas," the propri-
etor said immediately. "I wouldn't have recognized you without
Rick," he told me. "You've gotten your hair very ooh-la-la." He
wiggled his head. "You're beautiful."

"Anteater nose," I said.

"No, your face has grown into it. Now you call it queenly."

After Rick posted high score, slapping and jamming the controls with contemptuous grace, we ate our snacks on tall stools
in the rear corner, nearly dark, surrounded by slowly shifting

color fields of idle video screens. I almost repeated my question from the car. Surely Rick's thinking had gone beyond his answer; he must have plans. But, I remembered, talk about Dad was forbidden in the arcade. Instead I said, "I just thought of Monty collecting for St. Ann's."

"Oh, no!" Rick threw his arms and legs out, laughing. "The killer kids."

One day Rick and I were home from school alone when the doorbell rang, followed by heavy knocking.

"Who is it?" we said. The thuds continued.

Never open a crack until the person identifies himself, we'd been commanded. "Who is it?" we yelled. Silence. No footsteps.

Neither daring to leave the other to call the police, Rick grabbed his bat and I the poker. We stood at either side of the door, bellowing "Hello."

Through a gap in the curtain I saw a sleeve. The pattern looked familiar. Recklessly I tore aside the curtain. It was Monty, a deaf mute.

The story, I realized, was intended to reassure my brother, a classic things-aren't-as-scary-as-we-make-them.

On the drive home I pulled Rick over for an antique shop. My sprayed-stucco Tucson apartment needed some genuine old Wilmington, I said. Rick, in his Def Leppard sweatshirt and pummeled leather jacket, cupped porcelain shepherdesses in his hands as if they were baby birds, and chatted up the proprietress while I browsed, counting on intuition. I'm no connoisseur.

Rick spotted the plain, bowed-back wooden armchair, part of a display cordoned off with silk rope. "The bedroom. Perfect," I said. No one was looking. I sat in it. Roomy, and with red velvet cushions it would be comfortable.

" 'Windsor tavern chair,' " Rick read from the catalogue. "Sixty-seven dollars. That's not such a rip for a place like this."

"*Incredible.* Rick, what an eye you've got."

"I'll buy it."

"How?" He was out of a job.

"I've got some part-time. I want to. It'll be a memento."

"I love it," I said, standing to hug him. I checked the entry. "Circa 1750. This is sixty-seven *hundred*."

He grabbed the pamphlet. "To throw your ass in? Christ," he yelled. He kicked the chair. It sprang away from his boot, rebounded from the wall and onto its side.

Rick bolted.

The four legs pointed at me. The spindly ribs nestled into the stubbled carpet. The chair lay on the floor like a breach of natural law. I ran, too.

My last morning Dad asked me to walk him around the reservoir. "His pep when you're here, it's night and day," Mother remarked.

"Keeping busy, Claire?" Dad said. I was steering him across icy patches, hands at his elbows.

"Best job I've had." An L.A. law firm had rushed open a Tucson office, defending a megadeveloper against a titanic subcontractor. Desperate for help, they'd made me a legal secretary despite no previous experience. I am a quick study. Admitting that sleaze would rule, whoever won the case, we employees joked incessantly, uneasily. But my research was stimulating, the pay good, the lawyers cynical and funny. Beautifully dressed and groomed, they were like models from premium liquor ads.

"Two parents with half a brain equals a kid with a whole one," Dad panted. We rested.

"Last time I was here, Rick was living in Elsmere, with a girl," I said.

"I believe that's so, Claire."

I pressed. Shouldn't Rick find his own place? Couldn't he get on with Sabo Electric again? Was he dating?

"He's got the T-Bird," Dad said. "A car is less upkeep than a woman."

"Aw, Dad." I spanked his hand. "You can't talk like that in the '80's."

Because Rick had never left, he had become invisible to Dad. In grade school Rick biked to Dad's work sites. He quit high school, joining the paint crew full-time to keep the business afloat, just as Dad was preparing to sell out. Now Rick broke leases, lost jobs, always returning.

I flew in from Wilmington racing, unable to settle down. I'd had no personal life outside Jim, and Leah was the only person I could think to call. We made a date for Saturday morning, her beginning ballet class. I'd never taken dance in my life.

Tiptoeing onto the particle-board floor, we lurched through chains of plie-ing pink babies, a handful of adolescents. My butt and boobs bulged out of the saggy old leotard. Leah didn't shave her armpits. Repeated in wall-length mirrors, we were a spectacle. But Leah retained vestigial technique from childhood lessons, and my calves were so strong that my sautes impressed the ballet mistress. Stringy and brown, at least sixty-five, she dressed in black from wrists to ankles, catching her hair in an orange kerchief. Referring to herself in third person, she would say, "Madame Rifi is not pleased with port de bras today."

At the end of class Madame Rifi offered me a role in the spring recital, "Babes in Toyland."

"Thank God," Leah said. "I'm the Toymaker."

To celebrate our new stage careers we ate brunch at a trendy cafe. Leah complained about Eskison, who had been out past three on successive nights. She set a curfew and locked the door, but he pounded and rang. "'I don't have to be here.' He keeps saying it."

"Junk him," I said, snapping my fingers.

"Of course. Why didn't I think of that."

I spilled sprouts down my chin and front, and laughed and

laughed. It struck me as so funny that after a lifetime in men's company I had spent the morning among generations of women. It was like slinging aside a backpack at the end of a hike, the hard scrunched muscles loosening, expanding.

The recital clearly haunted Madame Rifi. Already in February she began teaching the class our dances. She devoted herself to the main parts, particularly the leads, a brother and sister played by the two oldest girls, who marked the choreography with spindly, clockwork competence.

Leah and I were expected to coach the Junior Corps, youngest age four. I'd not had to mind little girls since our family Thanksgivings and Christmases fifteen years before; Dad had withdrawn from holidays once he was sick. Simply trying to form the children into a line was impossible, their elbows and hips sticking out every which way. While Leah guided one at a time through the basic steps, the rest sat cross-legged, chewing their feet, or rolled, crashing into each other, giggling.

"Keep your places," I yelled, clapping my hands. Openly defying me, two ran across the studio and hid behind the water cooler.

Suddenly I was trembling, my concentration blacked out. I felt alone in the room, the rebellion inside my own head. The scattering children were parts of myself getting away from each other. And I was chasing, grabbing their arms, shouting, "What the hell do you think you're doing?" They burst out crying.

Over salad at our cafe I told Leah I was too ashamed to go back.

She shook her head. "Smile and nice them up, and they'll forgive. With little ones you can get away with murder, frankly. It only comes out later. Twenty years from now they'll snap and gun down a touring *Swan Lake*."

"I'm not myself. I think my brother's on drugs," I said, feeling again the bewilderment as I described the fallen chair, the mute legs poking at me. And it was Valentine's Day, I said, when Jim would have taken us to Mexico for our annual shrimp feast.

"Dear," Leah said, "you're one person I don't worry about. That's what's so wonderful about you." Everybody took drugs, she continued. "When I was Rick's age, I pickled myself in everything conceivable."

I admitted experience in that area myself.

"And here we are," Leah said. For that matter, she continued, Eskison dealt seasonally, to pay his tuition. Not that he'd go so far as to contribute toward rent. Last summer she'd made him get a job, and he drilled a hole through his hand.

Eyebrows raised, Leah stared over her fork at me. I challenge you to accept a fool like me, her expression said. So naturally I did.

I was sorry I yelled, I began. I was in a bad mood, I said, making a ridiculous mean face, pulling down my eyes and spreading my mouth with my fingers. The Junior Corps laughed, except for those two. I was extra attentive to them, manipulating their little hinged knees, rubbery arms, supporting their tummies on walkovers.

Leah, I noticed, treated rehearsal as playing. Demonstrating a step, she'd incorporate an outrageous error, snarling her legs, hopping on one foot. "No, *no,* Lili," the Corps howled—and performed the move flawlessly. Leah designated me the model of correctness. "Show her, Claire," the Corps insisted, cheering when I did, joining me. When the girls finally swarmed us, overexcited, punchy, hugging us, someone pushed, crying. Leah sat us down for circle games.

"You're incredible," I said later, as we ate.

"Experience. I raised three." Currently with their father, in Oakland. "After years of his hounding me, I said, 'O.K., you've got your chance. Take them.' Face it: He's remarried, dual-income family. This was before Eskison, I was loose ends. I was kind of moody, at the time, for being a parent."

Only once, weeks after, Leah flipped open her wallet snapshots. From under Leah's thick lustrous hair gazed Leah's intelligent brown eyes in a young woman, teenaged boy and girl. "The father must have no genes," I said. Leah smiled infinitesimally, for a second.

To reward their progress, Madame Rifi allowed the Junior Corps to rehearse in costume. But the starched chiffon skirts were a failure. During their big number, the March of the Toys, the material snagged, the Toys becoming entangled. Unaccustomed to their new dimensions, the girls constantly bumped, knocking the smallest down.

"The hell with it," Madame Rifi said, unpinning the skirts. And she redesigned the entire production. The Toys would wear plain black leotards. The March would progress from a serpentine meander across stage to a revolving circle. Then, single file, the Toys would stretch up their arms and sink to the floor.

"Toys are totemic," Madame said. "Beneath the surface, the March of the Toys has the ritualistic validity of anything in 'Le Sacre du Printemps.'"

Leah, the evil Toymaster, barelegged in sleeveless black leotard, would register ambivalence toward her misdoings by socking herself in the gut. As Mother Goose, I summoned nursery rhyme characters with alarmed twisting leaps.

Though Madame Rifi was a clown, her choreography for me was intuitive, a physical struggle with my anxieties, my chest and neck straining for height against the sideways wrenching of my arms. I practiced at home until completely drained.

"Babes in Toyland" was a smash. Brother and Sister whirled crisply. The Toys, in floppy yellow headpieces sewn by Leah in homage to youth's imperishable frivolity—so she convinced

Madame Rifi—toppled on cue, in rippling cadence, like dandelions before a mower. Leah gesticulated and doubled over. I sprang, adrenaline lifting me like a hand, my arms ricocheting around me like tetherballs, grunting.

At curtain call Madame Rifi kissed everyone, presenting not only the leads but Leah and me with bouquets of roses. The cast party disbanded quickly since most members were up past bedtime.

Leah and I drank sombreros. "These totemic straws stir with ritualistic validity," she said, and we laughed, but irresistibly we began moving on our barstools, tossing back and forth bits of our routines. We toasted each other—the Toys had come through. I kept my bouquet long after it dried, and so did Leah.

I wrote Rick during the spring, urging him to visit. I received a postcard of a pig with tricolored Mohawk slopping from a toilet. From library research Leah fed me articles and monographs on depression in ALS families. But all recommended counseling, and Rick would sooner have gone Moslem. Our whole family is that way.

Madame Rifi's disbanded for the summer.

Early on a Saturday Leah called, distraught. Eskison hadn't come in at all. I prescribed a hike. When I arrived, Eskison was on the line. "He's blubbering and stammering," Leah said. The new lover was his lab partner, nineteen years old. While I packed water and lunch, Leah kneaded her fingers on the couch.

The trail followed a canyon into the mountains. The June morning was deceptively mild until we switchbacked out of the streambed, and the heat turned Leah purple. At the first widening of the path she flagged me for water.

"I was teargassed in People's Park," she said aggressively, as if I were responsible. At my uncomprehending look, she said, "Berkeley, 1969. We were a mob, we had broken loose and the fences were going down. We were dangerous. Ecstatic." She paused. "And then the gas and clubs came in from the other side, and we were smashed into these knots of people. Beaten. Weeping." Her husband had been an organizer. "Good, dull man. Still at it, runs a co-op in Oakland. Good father. I'm a shit mother."

I croaked an obligatory dissent, and we trudged upward. On the loops below others toiled under colorful backpacks.

Leah kicked stones off the edge.

"Are you crazy," I yelled. The avalanche trickled downhill, missed.

"I'm such an asshole." Leah sat on a rock, slapping her face.

I grabbed her wrists. "Listen," I said. "You march up this mountain behind me and don't say one more fucking word."

It took hours. Emerging from the canyon, the trail bumped over hard, flat tableland, scented with juniper, before ascending through rhyolite pillars and Ponderosa. The last half mile was practically vertical. Our thigh muscles burned. We halted every few dozen yards for water. Finally we flung ourselves on the grassy summit.

Cloud shadows floated over the hazy pastel desert, which met billows of clouds at the horizon.

Leah shook her head, making awed noises in her throat. "You take such good care of me," she said, throwing her arms around my neck.

Astonished, I stroked her awkwardly. She was musky with fresh sweat, a smell I like.

"He'll be back, no question there," she said.

"No," I said, full of benign power. "He doesn't get the chance. I'll help you. You hold to it. Jim doesn't even know my address or phone."

Leah sat up. "Not everyone has your guts of steel. I'm a dry old stick. Who's got time to go looking?"

"You're so ridiculously beautiful," I said. The color in her cheeks had subsided to ruddy. Her damp bangs curled across her forehead. Despite threads of gray and lines at her chin, her skin was milky smooth, legs firm as a girl's, not a vein. She was the healthiest-looking miserable person I've met.

"He fucks a teenybopper now and then, what do I expect?" Leah said.

Lunch hit us like an anesthetic. Flattened on the warm grass, we slept.

We woke with cloud in our faces, thunder booming. As we stampeded down the trail, the downpour veiled us from each other, but I heard the sliding rattle of Leah's footsteps. Plunging out of control, yet charmed, I dodged boulders, leaping logs and roots. Ponderosa stands cut the pelting rain. The path turned to mush. We splattered around switchbacks, alongside gorges, not breaking stride until the parking lot. We had run continuously over an hour. Staggering rubberlegged, we whooped hoarsely, arms upraised.

Leah ripped open her shirt. Her small, perfectly round breasts streamed water. "Claire, I do. I feel cleansed of him," she said.

She refused to snap up for the ride home.

"What if a cop stops us, or a bus goes by?" I said.

"What if!"

I unbuttoned, too. Wipers singing, arms out the windows, shirts flapping, we cruised the drainage rivers that Tucson streets become. When we rounded the corner to Leah's block, dusk, Eskison's truck wasn't in the driveway.

"Please come in." Clutching her shirt together, Leah ran for the door, I behind her. After a quick ransacking for signs of his return, she said, in a small voice, "Well?"

I was shivering, from exhaustion mostly, though the cooler had chilled the air. "Come on," Leah said, leading me into the bathroom. We stripped and wrapped in towels. Sitting me on the edge of the bed, she brought us mugs of brandy. "Can you stay?" she said.

"I can't move." In a stupor I crept in beside her, skin to skin, and conked out.

When I woke, Leah's leg was draped over mine, hot and humid. Identifying the tickle of her pubic hair against my hip, I felt as if I were in a dream. While I was lifting off her leg, her eyes opened. Momentarily startled, they focused on me. Instead of separating, I rolled toward her, laying my arm against her back. Leah's eyes closed and, arms hugging her chest as they had while she slept, she squirmed hard against me, as if hollowing a place for herself. I soothed her with my hand. Her shoulderblades were so delicate they reminded me of fish bones. I rubbed in widening circles.

Jim's buttocks were smackable hairy islands. Leah's squashed in my hands, clenched into mounds. I ran my hand flat over her ass. With a little hitch in my stomach, I grooved my fingers, from behind, into the hair and cleft, brushed her thighs with my nails.

Leah's mouth pressed against mine, and the sensation of dream returned. We kissed so long, hardly moving our lips, that I became conscious of my neck, which seemed incredibly elongated.

Breaking apart, legs still entwined, we looked at each other. Eyes half-lidded, Leah traced my nipple with her pinky, thoughtfully joggled my breasts in her palms. Fearing the loss of what was happening, I drew her close, feeling her all along the front of me. We wriggled together. Sweat greased her body, and my hands over her were a blur. When our sweat-glued stomachs unstuck with a farting noise, we laughed only briefly. Leah's hand slid purposefully between my legs, but its movements there were a languid dragging back-and-forth of the knuckles. I came in waves that emptied me of everything. The brown tinge of the room was from inside me.

When I reached for her, Leah clamped her thighs around my hand, grinding herself against it. She twisted her hips toward me, pushed, arching her back. Struggling, head in the crook of my arm, she came, too.

We kicked off the sweltering sheets and lay legs apart, toes pointed out, so nearly identical: belly-button pools of sweat, pale bellies, clumps of pubic hair.

Leah got up, belted her robe. I found her in the kitchen, cracking frozen blocks of leftovers into pots. She plaited and undid the ends of her hair, spoke in sideways snatches. I read my signal to leave.

For an afternoon I was in love, with the ease of it all, remembering Jim, his bulky hurlings and our straining together, breathing like air pistol shots, his conscientious manipulations. Love, it suddenly seemed revealed, was the absence of heaviness, complication, dread. I was comfortable with what Leah and I had done. The moment of Leah's deciding to make me come was sweet to think about. I sunned in the lounge chair, dozing.

With the coolness at sundown fell the certainty, based on Leah's nervous, evasive send-off, that our lovemaking wouldn't be repeated.

"I can't believe it," she said when I called. "Claire, how did it happen?"

We were both under stress, she was angry at Eskison, I explained.

Leah coughed. "I've caught a cold."

I brought Nyquil and spent a desultory evening, bored with her, impatient to the point of hatred with her sneezes and nose-blows, grinding my teeth in martyrdom as I delivered encouraging statements. Boredom is always a mask for something more serious. Tonight, I discovered driving home, it was sadness.

After a week of halting phone conversations, we set lunch at our cafe.

"We can't let anything happen to this friendship," Leah said. We locked hands across the table.

"I had stage fright coming over," I said. "I felt like I was going to a summit meeting."

"It was fun," Leah said. "Our adventure. We'll be awkward for a few weeks, but that will wrinkle out."

"Iron out?"

Leah tapped her head, rolling her eyes.

Munching her croissant, she said, "Eskison showed up."

"And you drove him off, firing rapidly through the window."

"Natch." Leah slumped in the chair, laughing.

"Shit, congratulations." I tossed my garnish in the air. I appreciated her not boasting, as she would have done before, about the reason for her sleepless eyes.

We undertook friendship-fostering activities, Leah accompanying me to movies. On a spending spree in Mexico, arms laden with decorations for my apartment, we succumbed to feeling privileged and tall, flirting with sidewalk vendors and even the border guards. With Eskison I helped her renovate the house. For three weeks I left work directly for Leah's, put in eleven-hour Saturdays and Sundays. Knocking off, we tumbled in front of the TV and balanced cold Foster's on our knees.

Initially the site was a ruin and Leah's face was drawn. Through the bare picture window—Leah had canned the drapes —I would see her and Eskison again mounting the ladders even as I drove away.

In grub shorts and T's, sweat visors, Leah and I troweled spackle alongside each other. We oohed the newly exposed tongue-and-groove ceiling, which stained the color of oiled leather. The living room rose, spacious, solemn, mysterious, like a planetarium or temple. The bathroom gleamed, the salon of an ocean liner.

"You're part of this house for good, it's kind of nice," Leah said.

Passing a drugstore greeting card display, I halted at the bursting hearts, curlicued verse: "Darling, dee dee dee dee mine, dee, dee, dee, dee thine . . ." People really send these, I thought. I considered buying one for Leah but recognized the humor as unbridled, dangerous.

I flew to Wilmington, ostensibly for Dad's birthday, determined that Rick would return with me.

Rick and I were playing gin when Dad fell off the toilet, a thump that brought us running. He was sprawled against the magazine rack. As Rick lifted him onto the seat, I wiped him. His balls were gray.

"Vi," Dad yelled wheezily, gripping the railing.

Mother was in the kitchen, I said.

"Vi!" He was staring straight ahead.

I went for her.

Our birthday outing led through Amish country, immaculate white Pennsylvania Dutch farms measuring off tidy, abundant fields. Mother had stayed home, grateful, I'm sure, for time alone.

Rick piloted the big family Olds. Dad faced into the breeze, closing his eyes. After he fell asleep, Rick flattened the accelerator and we skimmed waves of green like a speedboat. The car jerked and swerved into a screeching skid. A tire had drifted into one of the ruts left by Amish wagons. Dad woke briefly, murmuring about a branch and rope. Shaking, I demanded to drive. Smiling fixedly, Rick raised his hands from the wheel and, keeping them high in surrender, slid out from the front and into the rear.

Every time I turned to speak, his hands shot up, palms out, alongside his ears; the same frozen smile appeared. About to lose it, gnawing my cheek, I pulled in at a village market, where I bought beer and wurst to go.

"Rick, you could fly back with me tomorrow," I said. "I'd rent a two-bedroom in the same complex, and we'd be moved in by next weekend. There's nothing more you can do for him."

"I can do this." Parting his lips, he squeezed out a cud of mashed wurst and sauerkraut, which leaked down his chin.

"That is re*volt*ing." My voice broke.

Rick laughed. "You should see your face."

"*Please* listen to me. Even I waited too long to leave." The summer after graduating from college, I was a bank teller, eating a
dozen percodan a day. My job was rote, the smile automatic, no
problem. Except for certain lapses. One shift a packet of twen-
ties became circus tickets. Was I supposed to be giving them
out to the kids? Twelve and under? I clicked back, but I caught
a flight to Tucson. I hadn't left home before, and Arizona had
never occurred to me, but it was far.

"Druggie, eh?" Rick said. "I'm surprised at you. I don't need
that shit."

The breeze turned cool and wet. We were driving home under
a late-afternoon overcast. Swarms of grasshoppers rose from the
fields and spattered against the windshield.

Dad sighed, rolling his head. "Smell that rain," he said.

"Look at this great sky," Rick said. "It's like a ceiling closing
around us and we're all together." He held up his fist. "Tight."

On the plane Rick pedaled his bicycle back and forth in my
head. Just when I thought he would burst through my skull, I
fell into a mini-nap, waking into a fantasy of Leah and me lying
sunbleached in some whitewashed corner of the world, Spain,
Greece. The shimmering glare rendered everything practically
invisible, a white field of light. Then Leah and Claire sat up,
naked to the waist, looking at me through dark glasses.

My first step onto the airport tarmac I knew I was turning
right around, going back. I'd need a week to settle my affairs.

At the apartment I riffled through the mail and listened to
my messages. "Claire," Leah's voice said, "Eskison's gone, took
his clothes, cleaned out." Weariness hit me, a pain between my
eyes. Postponing her, I watched TV and slept twelve hours.

After my long day trying to wrap up at the law office, Leah
welcomed me with a bottle of Kahlua. Perching on a stool in a
desert of spotted drop cloths, she was gravely composed.

"Oh, baby," I said.

"Nothing we haven't endured before. Persevere." Knocking back a tumbler of Kahlua in one swallow, she gave details. The nineteen-year-old lab partner was transferring to San Diego State, and Eskison had followed her to summer school. "Eskison was abject," Leah said. "He wanted my permission. I mean, I'd be damned."

By the cracking of the second bottle, she was singing medleys of pop and show tunes, substituting "fuck" for key verbs: "I'm going to fuck that man right out of my hair . . . Fuck! I need somebody. Fuck! Not just anybody . . ."

Her entire face was set in a wince. "I miss him being here, you know?" She threw herself sideways onto the floor. A snarl came through clenched teeth, her legs whipping. Terrified, I pinned her shoulders, grabbed her face, shook her, kissed her. "Stop, stop." Gradually her frenzy played out into little kicks.

I put Leah to bed and slipped in beside her. Throughout the night her thrashing jumped me awake. Morning, she paced aimlessly, licking her lips and making sucking noises. I canceled work and drove her to a therapist she'd seen pre-Eskison. I had to tell her I'd be in Wilmington indefinitely. She butted her head against the car window.

Leah had a pistol, the therapist informed me after the session, which must be relinquished immediately into my safekeeping.

"We're not talking about that kind of situation," I said.

My friend, he said, was in an extremely volatile state.

"This is such bull." I turned to Leah. Her face was smug, glittery, unrecognizable. Reflected in the receptionist's window I saw the outlines of our three heads together. It wasn't real. I should be in Wilmington, with Rick, and yet this mild, thin-lipped stranger, sport shirt casually open at the neck, was providing hotline numbers, detailing hospitalization procedures. It was as if I were in a theater and the movie beginning was the wrong one. I was stumbling across interminable knees, spilling popcorn, knowing that my movie was spinning in another room, and all the while these huge, hateful images were stamping themselves on my brain.

My send-off from the office amazed and moved me. The girls presented me with perfume and a crossword puzzle book. Roger, the lawyer with whom I worked most directly, assured me he considered my replacement temporary; such excellence couldn't be expected from another.

But once in the air I bottomed out on my failures with Leah, Rick. I was heading home to what? Get a job? Wring my hands in a corner? I couldn't affect anyone's life. I could only attend it.

After a morning delivering resumés to law firms, I was home, where Rick whipped a tennis ball against the wall, scooping grounders. Mother was giving Dad a bath, sloshes and murmuring coming through the door.

"Hi," I said into the receiver. "I'm thinking about you."

"Just finished swimming," Leah said. "I'm into my heavy aerobics endorphin rush. Ahh." The therapist was teaching her to regard suicidal impulses, panics, weeping attacks as simply distress. Ride them out and they would pass. "I imagine that you're watching, being proud of me."

"I can't stand that this is happening to you."

"Weirdhead Eskison" still called, from California, not even collect, to ask if she was O.K. "I tell him I'm completely on the rocks," Leah said.

I'd been a teller, first job available, for five weeks. Rick buzzed the drive-through lanes once, depositing a cricket in the pneumatic tube. It jumped on my arm when I opened the canister.

Leah's semester had begun, three algebra sections. She was getting by, a grinding existence directed at no particular end. The memory of us waving Madame Rifi's rose bouquets under a makeshift coffee-can spotlight was like a wonderful invention that was never going to be funded.

Rick was killed when a tire blew and the T-Bird, doing an estimated 90, rammed a concrete pillar. Mother called.

"Oh my God," I screamed, sobbing, falling against the teller box. "What's the matter? Are you all right?" crackled the intercom. Through the smudged glass a mouth opened, an arm waved at me.

When I ID'ed him the damage was to the back of his skull, and his neck was broken, which I couldn't see. The bruise across his eyes looked very painful, though, and I couldn't believe it didn't hurt. I kept flinching at the thought of it, wanting to press a cold cloth against it.

I would live in Wilmington, I decided. I never should have left, and now it was too late, but staying was the only right choice.

Leah had booked a flight east before I convinced her our family couldn't cope with an outsider.

Overly generous, I gave rides home to a waspish backbiting teller who lived miles across town. I let a loan officer, a bored sexual technician with wavy black hair and a mustache like a streak of Magic Marker, fuck me at his apartment during lunch. I owed everybody.

Immediately following work I helped Mother cook. Soon it was dark by my arrival, a frosty halo around the porch light. After eating, Mother washed, I dried. She knitted in the den, Dad watched the screen, blanket around his knees.

I was splurging on a daily six of good English beer. Having forgotten, I was reminded, by myself, of that puffy, pallid Northeast fleshiness that makes nice clothes a complete waste. I bought suits a security guard would wear.

Leah was calling. "Here's the plan. The day you fly in I make scallops in champagne sauce. You soak in the tub, hot, to soften you up for . . . massage! At least an hour, to rub out all that damage. Then you sink back in the pillows while Leah presents Marx Brothers. Steve Martin. Laugh. Empty your head."

"Sounds really great," I said. Good-bye, good-bye.

Rick came to me.

I was hanging out regularly in his bedroom. Pause at dresser. Pause at window. Sit at foot of bed. This particular night I didn't switch on the lamp but squatted, holding my knees, in the dark. Then there was a light just outside my peripheral vision. But the light was more a presence, as if the air had been replaced by something purer and colder. I pushed my head deeper into my arms, scared and glad, rocking slightly. "Rick," I said, and felt an answering warmth.

Nothing more happened. After an hour or so, satisfied, I went to bed.

Leah: "What worries me is that I'm holding myself together until you're here, and then I'll go to pieces."

"Don't be goofy," I snapped.

I couldn't wait to polish off the evening beers, for Mother to complete her private crying, Dad to slip down into the couch. I took my place on Rick's carpet. We were there together.

A Sunday afternoon I played his records and emptied his shoe-box of baseball cards. I read his class notes, mostly doodling—a cross-eyed George Washington, centipede crawling up his nose. I tried to envision the classroom the day of that drawing, yellow-painted brick, the teacher's bald pink dome. Restless Butt, in plaid shorts, scooching in her seat.

"Finally laid her at a party when she was drunk, in the back-yard," Rick had told me.

"Real aristocrat, that one," I'd sniped, faithful to our tradition.

"At least she's not a psycho like your Vinnie Toglia . . ."

An unbearable emptiness invaded me, moved outside, surrounding me. Walking from window to window, I punched out every pane of glass in the room.

Blood ran along my arm as I drove to Emergency. My skin prickled. It was the kind of winter when the snow sifts down the same gray-white as sky and ground, no sun for weeks. I was following strings of taillights, and when they braked, it was a chain reaction, flashes zeroing in on me like dotted lines. I was part of a natural involuntary process, no need to depress the brake pedal, the car would stop by itself. Calmly I watched the space shrink between me and the forward car. A fraction too late my foot did go down and the locked wheels skimmed my car across the ice, kissing the bumper ahead.

Leah's next call, she said, "If I was dead, at least my kids could explain to themselves why they were packed off."

"I can't listen to this kind of talk." My voice was shrill. I hung up. Without my intending to break with her, I didn't speak to Leah again while I was in Wilmington.

Dad was choking more often, and we moved the suction machine from the kitchen to the dining room. Physically needier after Rick, he liked to fall asleep against me while I stroked his hands.

Roger the lawyer was on the phone, apologizing for the intrusion, giving his condolences. He was joining a partnership in San Francisco and wanted me to accompany him. "No one else could run my office," he said.

Incredulous, not knowing what I was saying, I joked, "What a coincidence. Bank of Delaware is transferring me to Paris, and I can't order in French. Parley voo?"

"I'm serious," he said. "I'll start you at two-and-a-half what you made in Tucson."

"Roger, I'm levitating." It was true, since hearing his casual surf's-up California voice, I'd been spiraling upward. Though fighting to stay put, I was rushing higher at incredible velocity. "Yes," I said. "I'm going, I'm going."

Mother's face closed as if a curtain had dropped. I promised to send money toward live-in help, which I've done.

"I can't understand this one, Claire," Dad said. "It's a heavy blow."

Putting over in Tucson to liquidate my possessions—meager as they were, more a case of erasing my tracks—of course I had to include Leah. I gave her most of the clothes. We're about the same height. She invited me swimming at the next-door neighbor's, a ludicrous Tucson March day, 91 degrees. "I've got to show you my new suit," Leah said, a pink Spandex. She was bony. Diving in, she scrambled, dripping, onto the deck. "Look. It gets transparent," she said, pirouetting. She was queerly naked, as if shrinking from her own skin.

In San Francisco my wardrobe ran to puffed sleeves and balloon skirts, in which my head and body dwindled. I felt suspended like an airy, diaphanous insect. After presiding over a revolving door of roommates, I moved in with Roger. We'd begun with weekend drives through the redwoods, with his tape boxes, forty-eight in each. Roger likes everything, Beethoven, 101 Strings, metal, Admiral Bailey—some obscure reggae discovery. I'd cry. Roger's copper hair refused to muss even with the windows down, wind eddies madly chasing our candy-bar wrappers.

I still feel as if I'm living in the silence following a noise so loud that the quiet is shocking, not to be believed.

Gradually I've allowed Roger to lavish indecent sums on me. Twice he's flown us to Europe. To shed my accumulated blubber I've taken up jogging with him. It's lovely, at daybreak, to pound the hills, the city below muffled in clouds.

I like Roger. He's taken the most marvelous tours, the Sahara, volcanoes in Indonesia, Alaskan glaciers. He won't pick a favorite but says all are worthwhile.

Leah was here last week, staying with her older daughter, who spent Christmas in Tucson. Homesick, the girl may transfer to the University of Arizona. "Her father is so virtuous, it gives her hives," Leah said. The other two are still angry, she said, although at least they're telling her so.

When Leah called for directions, I braced myself with a hard run to the end of the pier. Damp from my shower, I tried different looks in the mirror, sand-cast silver necklace, T-shirt, jeans, flip-flops.

The person swinging up the walk was dressed in a peach silk blouse, gray wraparound skirt furling about her legs.

"Tummy in, ripcage oudt," Leah barked in Madame Rifi's suspect European accent. We clipped our posture, smiling. In my fantasized reunions she threw herself frantically into my arms, I gently whisking the hair from her face. The real Leah's hug, firm and close, released smartly. "Man must moonlight as an oil sheik," she said, glancing around the place. Roger was in L.A. for the weekend.

I served us wine on the porch. We did a location chat, parking, the fog, the wind.

"You could tell me why you didn't call," Leah said.

"I'm sorry. I thought you might take the change-of-address card as an invitation."

"I couldn't be first. I've been such a bloodsucking leech."

Ducking that, I asked, "Seeing anyone?"

"Claire, I haven't been with a soul since Eskison. I have to attribute that to you," she said, "your cutting me off, sort of. That was tough medicine, and I don't know if I forgive you for it, but it was good medicine."

"I'm sorry," I repeated.

"You had your reasons, honey, God knows." She crossed to me and we embraced again, this time a sticky one.

Through a bottle of Chardonnay, Leah told me that she swam, took the neighbor kids for chili dogs. The past election she'd volunteered for two local candidates. "One for two." After test-marketing her quilted pillows, a mall boutique had picked up the line. "Whoopie shit," she said, twirling her finger. "Whoopie cushions."

Arranged in the deck chair she was nearly composed, only her hands balling and releasing.

"You've fleshed out," I said. "Nicely, I mean."

"Now that I don't want, natch, there's the carpenter who sanded my floor, all my students are in love with me . . ."

Captivated by her familiar lilt, I thought, hasn't she become exactly who I want? Though I continued to talk—gesturing at a pelican flapping comically—I was flushed, with the cool hollowness that precedes tears. But I am so light now, this insubstantial hovering—love is as palpable as dirt filling your mouth, glass pricking your skin. I poured more wine, knowing the trembling would pass.

But Leah! Head tilted, laughing, arm gracefully outstretched —how can a person cease being who she's always been? Miracles, all kinds. Pathology arrests itself. A heart knotted with the effort of love slips into love like a bar of soap. A boy sits in a tree, heels kicking against the limb, and as you watch he falls to the ground. Friendships end.

FROM THE PHILIPPINES

Deirdre's Philippine snapshots were late. Every day they failed to arrive, Deirdre's friend Curtis told her, she grew dizzier. Her gray eyes glittered. Her freckled complexion flushed pink. The soft waves of her auburn hair burst into a fiercely becoming curly frame around her head. She talked incessantly, though not about the Philippines, since by now everybody but Curtis refused to hear about it. She had spent a semester and summer there, as an exchange student.

When the final bell rang, Deirdre edged down the ramp, books clamped to her chest, in a surge of 2,500 other high school students. She felt assaulted by bulges—the boys' prodding crotches, the girls' nipples encircled by blonde flips and Izod alligators. Deirdre hated their touching her. Her first months home after the Philippines, she'd needed only to close her eyes to be shinnying up a date palm with Chacho or ladling Mama's fish stew, her back to the warm oven. Now she felt in the midst of her recurrent dream: waking on a beach that came alive, a moving carpet of crabs, feathery and spiky, intimate with all of her. As the students squeezed down the ramp, a boy pushed himself against her buttocks. Deirdre swung her looseleaf binder back in a hard uppercut. She heard a grunt. When she knelt at her locker, a girl was saying above her, "Who would you kick out of bed, Erik Estrada or Sugar Ray Leonard?"

"Good-bye Erik," another answered. "Give me brown sugar every time. Who would you kick out of bed, Billy Zoom or Billy Idol?"

"*Whom*," Deirdre said. "Wignorant itches. *Whom* would you kick out of bed. Think of womb. That shouldn't be any trouble for you."

Home, no mail. Her father squirmed in his armchair and sipped from a highball glass, watching TV. He'd sat there for eight years, since rheumatoid arthritis had forced his retirement from City Maintenance. The living room belonged to him. No one else was allowed to use it.

Deirdre filled her silver pint flask from the half gallon of Seagram's in the kitchen and drove into the hills.

Thickets of mesquite gave way to saguaro forest as she hiked up the mountain. Below her, trails meandered through muted green desert in a scene as delicately complex as a Japanese water-color. Soon Deirdre was in the Philippines. At first she couldn't capture the matter-of-factness of true memory. The tropical vegetation was impossibly shaggy, the colors blaring purples and greens. Then she was swimming in slow motion, water flowing over her back. Crisp stems of water hyacinth parted beneath her fingers, the petals brushing her face. Her host Filipino family— Mama, Papa, Chacho, and the three sisters—flitted through the trees, their white underwear iridescent. Afterwards they lay on the bank, Chacho asleep, his head on Deirdre's knee.

Swallowing from her flask, Deirdre sat against the trunk of a palo verde and put her hands to her temples. By almost closing her eyes she could see Chacho as a mountain hovering in the distance, huge. His lowered lids were sloping faces of rock, his mouth a soft crease in the earth. Floating over the desert, the Chacho-mountain swept back and forth, erasing the gray and glass bits of the city, the cars with hundreds of setting suns reflected off their roofs, the chatter of her high school halls.

With delight, Deirdre recalled reading Kahlil Gibran aloud

with Chacho: "When you part from your friend, you grieve not; for that which you love most in him may be clearer in his absence, as the mountain to the climber is clearer from the plain."

She walked back down the trail into the dusk, singing. After she could no longer see them, she could hear her feet on the stones. The long curve of lights marking the boundary of the city was the Manila shoreline. The far mountain range, absorbed into the dark, was the ocean. A few birds, she thought, would still be flying over the obsidian water.

In the kitchen at home, her mother gave her carrots to wash and peel, broccoli to trim. Deirdre held the lumps of vegetable under the streaming tap. She felt dazed, and the light hurt her eyes. Her mother hurried from stove to refrigerator to counter to oven. From long practice, the two cooperated well and had little need to talk. Mrs. McGuire seldom spoke, as a matter of habit. Turning from the sink with her pots of vegetables, Deirdre bumped her mother, carrying meat loaf in a pan. The broccoli tipped onto the floor.

"Sorry, Mom."

"We'll wash it. We won't tell anyone."

Deirdre giggled, but her mother already was past, opening the oven door.

Deirdre set the table and, when dinner was ready, served her young sisters. They were beautiful and untrustworthy; Deirdre constantly covered for them. One stole money from her mother's purse. The other would not do *anything,* not clean her room, help with the dishes. She cried when asked to put away her clothes.

Deirdre brought her father a plateful of food. "They're in it now," he said, pointing to the TV. "No one's going to get them out of this one."

His arm knocked the highball glass to the floor. "Get me another, sweetheart," he said.

"Ha, ha," Deirdre said. Often, despite her sharing the Seagram's, her urge was to spit in his liquor. Resisting, she would feel sick with herself for the thought. She returned to the dining room, sat down, and began to eat. But her father yelled until her mother made him a 7 and 7. Furious, Deirdre said nothing for the remainder of the meal.

Curtis was late picking her up. Deirdre walked back and forth in her room, reading Gibran's "On Friendship" from an imitation parchment scroll, a gift from Chacho. The JV game had gone into double overtime, Curtis explained when he arrived. He was the school paper's assistant sports editor. Deirdre tucked the scroll in her back pocket, and they drove toward a boondocker in the desert, drinking rum.

"I never told you the weirdest thing that happened to me with Gloria," Curtis said. Deirdre and Curtis had carried on their six-week friendship by exchanging monologues, hers on the Philippines, his on Gloria. Curtis was driving fast up First Avenue, and badly, as usual. Twice he yanked the car back from the dirt shoulder. Sometimes he drove with his right hand on the wheel and his left waving out the window, sometimes with his left on the wheel and his right arm around Deirdre.

A month ago, he told her, just before the breakup, he'd sneaked the car by pushing it out the driveway and down the block, then gone to Gloria's. He woke her by tapping on the bedroom window.

"She had on her nightgown, which was just a little lace here and here, and even in the dark I was just thiiis close to seeing her through it." Curtis had admitted that he tried to look down Deirdre's blouse and the back of her jeans whenever possible. "She put on her fur coat and came out the window."

On their way to the desert, she'd tickled his neck and stuck her tongue in his ear, Curtis said, but when they parked, it was the same as always: neck, arms, and legs below the knee, O.K. Shoulders and back outside her clothes, O.K. Period. "We're kissing and I'm going crazy, and all of a sudden I realize I'm embracing, stroking, really digging my fingers into this thick fur. I feel like I'm making love to a big muskrat. I ask her, hey, whose perverso movie is this?"

"I don't know what's wrong with Gloria. If I weren't the Frigididity Queen, I'd be raping you every second," Deirdre said kindly. Curtis might have been called peculiarly handsome, tall and slender, with pointy features, thick white-blond hair, and dark circles under his eyes.

"Say 'frigidity,' " Curtis said.

"Frigididity." It was Deirdre's policy to fracture words suggesting sex.

"Say 'tits.' "

"Bazoozums."

"Say 'ass.' "

"Hindnickels."

"Excellent. Say 'vagina.' "

"Virginia."

"That's the girl. I was thinking, the reason they haven't sent the pictures is probably because it's harvest time or something."

"That was November," Deirdre said. "It's almost Christmas." She didn't want to talk about the mail. After three letters a week from Chacho, now no letters in five weeks.

From the top of the rise in the dirt road they saw the party, two bonfires in a dry swimming pool, part of an abandoned, reputed Mafia resort of the '50's. A couple of dozen natty teenagers danced to a boom box between the fires.

Deirdre soon was drunk again, with the accompanying tension that left her face lopsided and pugnacious. She was concentrating on Chacho's theory of sex: with abstinence, the sexual fluids would rise up the spine into the head, creating a dynamo of spiritual energy. "The face glows," he'd said, "like yours." While the tape was being changed, she climbed onto the diving board. Shadows of flames played over the pool like a negative of sunlight on water. The board felt very high, and slender like a bending reed.

"What do any of you know about friendship?" she said. "The Filipinos understand friendship. Your *kasama* is your friend for life! *Pingsarili*—you would translate that as 'privacy.' That's what I used to think. But Pilipino has no word for privacy. *Pingsarili* is like loneliness. Imagine a people whose word for privacy means loneliness. Friendship!"

"Oh, Christ, Deirdre," someone said. A bottle broke against a far wall.

From her back pocket, Deirdre pulled the scroll of Gibran's "On Friendship." After reading, she replaced the parchment in her pocket and recited the whole from memory.

The others began singing loudly.

"Friendship is staying up all night on the beach, just talking," Deirdre shouted. "Friendship is giving everything, your secrets, your voice, your language, and getting everything in return. Friendship is touching for love, not tutti-frutti. 'Let there be no purpose in friendship save the deepening of the spirit.'"

The diving board sagged and bounced. Below Deirdre, her companions' faces looked as remote and featureless as pebbles. "Come sit with me," Curtis was saying, and, his arm around her shoulders, he led her to the pool steps.

How many acres did the family farm? he asked. What was the growing season? What were the major crops of the Philippines? His pointed nose and sharp chin darted toward her with intense earnestness. Deirdre wasn't fooled. She knew he quizzed her to disguise his boredom with the Philippines. She didn't care. Boring everybody gave her a sense of accomplishment and pride. Curtis at least tried to be interested.

Deirdre explained the planting of rice. She remembered ambling home astride the carabao, led by Chacho, how she could lean forward and grip the animal's sweeping horns, like tremendous handlebars, and rub the forehead, broad as a slab of moss-covered mahogany. Chacho's brown feet squashed into the mud, guiding her through green rice plants and rich brown earth, paddies that seemed endless.

"Do the women ever work in the fields topless?" Curtis asked.

"The old grannies, maybe, in the hills."

"Did you ever work topless?" His forehead contracted into cobwebbed lines, his eyes squinted eagerly.

"Mother of God," she said.

"My dick hangs down the left leg of my pants, and I notice that everyone else's is on the right," Curtis blurted. He rolled and lit a joint, but something was wrong and one side of the paper flared up like a jet of natural gas. "My guess is that it won't function properly. Go in crooked. Gloria knows her sex, she would have caught that right off. There's the problem."

After they'd gone together six months, Gloria had told Curtis she'd slept with a quarterhorse trainer she picked up at the track. The man, a Canadian, moved on with the racing circuit, but Gloria said since she was in love with him there was no point in seeing anyone else.

"Unzip," Deirdre said. "Show me."

"What?"

"Come on."

Curtis turned his back to the bonfire, hunched forward, lowered his fly, and cupped his hand around, without touching, his exposed penis.

"It's fine," Deirdre said. "No problem."

"But how would you know?"

"My father leaves his lying around carelessly sometimes. Yours is much more appealing, believe me."

Curtis finished his smoke. "This makes me nervous," he said. "I'm going to move around." He hopped the pool steps two at a time and began loping along the rim of the pool, circling it twice with high, floating bounds. His white hair stood on end, settled, rose, fell. The black circles made his eyes look enormous in his white face.

On Deirdre's front porch, Curtis suddenly kissed her on the lips. Startled, she allowed his tongue in her mouth. Her mouth gaped open, slack, until he put his hand on the seat of her jeans. She stiffened. Her saliva took on a metallic tinge. She thought of his hands in fur, a dead animal, his fingers breaking through desiccated skin and tufts of hair. A line of teenagers embraced, the girls in their pleated skirts crumbling, clothes collapsing to the concrete floor of the swimming pool. "Good night," Deirdre said. Pushing off Curtis's chest, she backed through the door.

Her father sat in the dark facing the gray slush of the TV screen. The pale light traveled up his legs, to his open fly and his penis, which pointed straight at his head. True as a compass needle, Deirdre thought. She hurried by.

Sitting on her bed, chin in hand, she thought of how Chacho, when he talked most seriously to her, would lie on his elbow and pluck at whatever was beneath him—grass, reed matting, sand. He had long black lashes. His eyes were soft; if she touched them, they would feel like the bodies of bees. Beauty in her life, Deirdre reminded herself, was a sign of favor, and Chacho was beautiful.

Deirdre woke at four in the morning to go to the bathroom. The kitchen light was on. Her father's armchair was empty, so he was spending the night in the master bedroom. Her mother, naked except for a black lace bra, an old birthday gift from her father, stood by the kitchen sink. Deirdre retreated into the shadow of the living room. She hadn't seen her mother naked that she could remember. Her mother reached for the cutting board and laid it on the counter. She turned, passed from Deirdre's view. The refrigerator door opened, shut. Her mother brought bread, a head of lettuce, mayonnaise, and luncheon meat to the counter. She spread mayonnaise on the bread.

Her belly and buttocks were round and white, too soft, even baggy. Afraid, feeling unbearable tenderness, Deirdre ran into the kitchen. Her mother shrieked. On her knees, Deirdre embraced those soft parts of her mother, pressed her face against them, the fluff of pubic hair.

"How can you let him have this?" she said. "How can you give it to him?"

Her mother, frozen, holding the knife and a slice of ham, stared at her. Then her eyes, as large and clear as Deirdre's, but blue, shifted vaguely around the room. She stepped free and returned wearing a robe.

"*Go to bed,*" she said. Deirdre stood, wanting to resist, but the robe stymied her. She could think of nothing to say.

To help herself sleep, Deirdre remembered wrestling Chacho's sisters in the pond. The girls clambered over her back, and she toppled forward. Chacho's arm shot around her waist, breaking the fall, and the tower of people collapsed on Papa and Mama on the bank. For a moment, the children squirming over her, Papa grunting underneath, Deirdre hadn't wanted to move, to leave the warm, wet flesh against her skin. The tangle rolled over on itself. The girls yipped. "Yaaah," said Chacho. "Ou ou ou," Papa said, punching and prodding the mass of flesh as if molding a great ball of dough. Smelling again their moist, common scent, Deirdre drowsed.

Friday there were no letters. Deirdre went to bed early and slept until Saturday noon.

It was time to check the mail. Her father waved. Cheerleaders were kicking long diagonals across the TV screen, the tips of their feet disappearing beyond the edge of the small picture tube.

Outside, a kite, rising on the unseasonably warm breeze, showed red against a fat bank of clouds. A packet from the Philippines lay in the mailbox. Deirdre slit the envelope with her fingernail and unfolded Chacho's note. He apologized for the delay. Papa had forgotten to send in the film, and then processing had taken longer than anyone could have imagined. He apologized for not having written. He was engaged to be married. The girl was a Christian Chinese, daughter of a grocer with connections to a department store chain in Manila. Chacho had never spoken to her. Papa and Mama were very enthusiastic, and he must obey their wishes. It was difficult for him to tell her this. He would write more later. He closed *"Iniigib kita"*—I love you.

The kite dipped in the pale sky. The bright winter sun seemed to have leached color from everything—house, trees, the bicycle on the lawn. Deirdre refolded the note and with great care tried to put it in her shirt pocket. The shirt had no pockets. Deirdre let herself into the house. She saw her father's bladelike face, small ears tight against his crew cut, the shriveled, twisted feet, and hatred clenched her stomach. She locked the bathroom door behind her, feeling enclosed in hatred like a vault. Sitting on the edge of the tub, she scraped her father's razor across her wrists until blood dripped onto the white porcelain. Then she began to cry. Running the bathwater to hide the sound, she staunched the blood with a washcloth. The wounds were only shallow scratches.

She called Curtis. He was covering a basketball invitational in Phoenix, because the sports editor was sick, he said, and of course she could come.

Wearing a long-sleeved blouse with frilled cuffs over the Band-Aids, Deirdre sat against the door in Curtis's front seat. Curtis smoked a joint, seeds sizzling and popping as they chugged along the freeway in his '51 Plymouth. The night before, he'd taken speed and lain awake reconstructing every minute he'd spent with Gloria. For an hour and a half he delivered the history to Deirdre, jerking the steering wheel back and forth in time to the music, cursing cars that passed them—"Dog's ass. Carnal intimate of rats."

Deirdre refused the puffs he offered. Watching his face, the most expressive, she realized, that she'd ever seen, she made a fascinating discovery. There was a wonderful beauty in the harshness of that face. Deirdre felt odd. Each moment was fragile, elongated. She couldn't remember where she lived, the number of her house, or what it looked like. The desert outside her window was unfamiliar. She couldn't judge if it were pretty or drab.

A swerve of the car threw his cigarettes on the floor. When she bent to retrieve them, he asked what was in her pocket.

"My photos." Deirdre broke the seal on the envelope and removed the prints. They were stiff colored artifacts in her hand. Chacho cutting green peppers into likenesses of the family, Papa with his cigar and big ears, Mama's bun and wide skirt, Chacho's floppy pandanus hat, Deirdre's backpack like a hump. Deirdre and Chacho reciting his Pilipino translation of "On Friendship," their mouths open exactly the same width on the same word. The sisters catching a frog. Chacho and Deirdre, late for Mass, running down a pink dirt path overhung with gray-green foliage, feet barely blurred. Each held the other's hat in place, his hand on her white lace chapel cap, her hand on his pandanus.

Deirdre tossed the photos on the seat. "You can look at them later," she said.

Curtis glanced at her, said nothing, and lit a joint.

Early for the game, they drove down a broad, shady boulevard. Above the treetops, a violent pink and orange sunset flamed the glass of a double-decker mall, the Phoenix smog curling like smoke.

Curtis needed more cigarettes. A series of turns took them into a black ghetto. Children popped wheelies on their bikes. People talked in doorways. The buildings were dingy and decayed. A tattered billboard showed an airplane flying into a glass of beer. Lying against the brick wall of a lounge, a man threw a tennis ball in the air, catching it without changing the position of his hands.

"Brrr, this is sad," Curtis said. "I shouldn't feel good in a place like this, but I do. Isn't that terrible? But Gloria and I were so close when we were sad. When she was depressed, she'd call, and we'd want so much to be together, but it would be too late at night and we couldn't. It was a sweet thing. I love her so much," he said, banging his hands on the steering wheel. "That's why I wanted to touch her. It would have been enough to feel the skin of her back. I always wondered if she has a nice back. That's important to me."

"I'm sure she does," Deirdre said. "Gloria has lovely bones."

"What's wrong with me? Six months, and then the first time she meets this Canadian horse mugger—I hate Canada. I read the hockey box scores every day to see the Canadiens lose. I want them to lose every one of their games."

"It makes me angry that Gloria treated you so badly. She needs a good kick." Deirdre's voice rose. She was trembling.

Curtis looked at her again. "Do you want a drink? We could have someone buy us a bottle."

Deirdre shook her head.

The gym was like an old hangar of yellow wood. Deirdre studied the rows of bleachers. Their existence seemed arbitrary. She might look away and back, she thought, and half would be gone. It was all a matter of pure chance. The buttocks of the players looked like sea sponges. Deirdre was unaware of the action until midway through the fourth quarter when, their team ahead by twenty points, Curtis lit a cigarette.

"Idiot," she said. "Do you want to get thrown out?" She crushed it on his bootsole.

Only when they were on the freeway home did Deirdre re-member, "Chacho is getting married."

"No," Curtis said. "I don't believe it. Oh, honey." He squeezed her arm tightly.

"We said we were never going to get married. Everly-Neverly Brothers never." Though she'd drunk nothing, her tense jaw pulled her face lopsided. Bare sticks of growth flashed by in the headlights. The vastness and emptiness of the desert sky, with its dull distant stars, terrified her. "He doesn't know her. He doesn't like her."

"Chacho must be miserable. He'd do anything to see you before it happens."

"I think I'm going to put my head in your lap," Deirdre said. She lay on her back, knees huddled against the seat. Curtis fingered her hair and stroked her cheek.

After a few miles, she unhooked her bra and put Curtis's hand inside her blouse. The weight of his hand made her feel the motion of her breast, vibrating with the hum of the engine. She felt the car decelerate and stop, the engine dieseling. She opened her blouse to Curtis and looked at him. He gazed at her without blinking. He was barely smiling, but the corners of his black-rimmed eyes turned down and his forehead was deeply lined. Covering her breasts with his hands, he bent to kiss her.

Deirdre averted her face. "None of that," she said. "Go ahead. A gift." Muscle knotted her jaw. Her teeth were clenched. She unfastened the buttons of her jeans and arched her back to strip herself. She heard part of Curtis bang against the steering wheel as he lowered himself onto her. It wasn't their bodies touching, Deirdre thought, but only a bridge from her to him.

Curtis's boots scuffed against the door. Occasional passing headlights swept across the interior of the car. Deirdre tried to hear Chacho's voice speaking of the sexual juices' ascent up the spine, their opening like a flower in the head, tried to see his hands illustrating the expansion of energy. But instead all she could see was a woman, not herself, yet leaving her body, racing into the glare of traffic. Holding her long, white, ugly breasts in her hands, the woman thrust them into the headlights, against windows of the passing cars. Metal grazed her. Headlights bore down on her. She lunged and dodged among the cars while the traffic broadened, a half dozen lanes wide, a dozen, a river of yellow lights. Now she was struck, broken on a hood, tossed to a roof, thudding from fender to door to bumper to windshield, flung from lane to lane. Deirdre's heart slammed against her chest and her breath tore in her lungs.

"It's O.K.," Curtis was saying. She was lying on the floor. His arms were under her, lifting her towards him. "Take it easy. You jerked right off the seat, that's all. We were already done. I got out in time."

Deirdre's naked body felt gray and dead in a film of moisture. To herself she smelled like the clots of dust in a vacuum cleaner.

"You look so wonderful," Curtis said. His face was smooth, lines at last relaxed. He kissed her breasts and draped her clothing over her. She allowed him to kiss her lips.

Driving home, Curtis said, "I have a vision of the Philippines." He described a long sweep of beach, ocean a blinding blue, thatched huts, and hundreds of brown people making love. Like bundles of driftwood, they were strewn along the sand, receding into the distance until they were only dots.

Deirdre's mind was blank, and so she saw only Curtis's couples, arranged symmetrically like a pattern for giftwrap, rolling by on an endless sheet.

Curtis walked her to the porch, pressing her hand. As she opened the door, a streak, a yellow ribbon of clashing noise and light, entered with her, but it faded. The living room was dark. Looking toward her father's chair, she saw that he had slipped to the floor. Suddenly she wanted everything to be different, that he would be healthy again, that she could even remember him healthy. But her memory of that time was always vacant. She lifted him by his armpits and set his stiff back into the hollow left by his years of sitting. He batted at her weakly.

In her room, Deirdre concentrated on the image of Curtis's wondering face, a new emblem. She couldn't lie down. Instead she found she must sit upright, knees drawn to her chest, while the yellow river of noise and light roared around her bed until morning.

In a Landscape Animals Shrink to Nothing

"Mouth gaping! Eyes bulging! Out of the water, burned, eaten up." Boehm spread the foil and jabbed the crisp skin of the snapper with a fork. "That's how I feel when I look at you."

Olivia, shucking corn, said nothing. Hunched, her small breasts in her bikini top drooping with a weight Boehm could almost feel in his palm, she ripped the fine blonde tassels that reminded Boehm of her own hair, and dropped them into a hole in the sand. Her concentration, teeth nibbling the curve of her underlip, made Boehm nervous. She would be thinking of her bare new apartment, her choices in decor, of the last truckload of boxes stacked in their living room.

Boehm clenched his eyes shut as if in pain, mushing the snapper with his fork, whipping the flesh like meringue. The fish's elegant shape was destroyed.

Keeping the smashed pulpy section for himself, Boehm served the fish. He reclined his beach chair and swigged from the mezcal bottle. Olivia had stopped drinking hours before because soon she would be taking her sleeping pills for bed. They were stupefyingly potent, illegal, and since her announcement that she was leaving Boehm she'd been unable to sleep without them.

"Even with that corn you've got a system," Boehm said. "You

do three ears in the time it would take me to do one. You're so intelligent. It's never bothered me that you're more intelligent than I am. I've learned from you."

"I don't accept that from you. You're a bright man, Steve." Olivia squatted, her back to Boehm, setting corn in the coals.

Bahia Umichehueve was blue, curved like a lens. Two islands, bristling with huge, weird cardon cacti and glazed with pelican guano, lay at the exact center. From time to time the surface of the water was broken by flying fish. Boehm was reminded of a map in a childhood favorite, *The Golden Book of Great Explorers,* showing the cobalt blue ocean surrounded by crudely drawn lumps for mountains, and in the foreground, gamboling fish with human faces.

The beach, which Boehm remembered five or six years before teeming with drunken, near-naked American students and slow-walking, embarrassed American fatties, was virtually empty. A cleaning detail of village children was at work. Beside Boehm a family from Guadalajara, the only other guests at the hotel, read newspapers and magazines. The parents and their three children were dressed in enveloping bathing attire made of a nubbed, rubbery material. The children had insisted on taking their yearly vacation in Las Playas, the man had explained, though the area was ruined. The climate was fine and the water a delightful warm temperature, like mineral baths. Boehm had nodded, as if understanding that the area was ruined, and why.

The children dashed into the mild surf. Watching them spin and collide on their red and yellow plastic rafts, Olivia said, "They have such beautiful, perfect little bodies." Squinting into the setting sun, parted lips exposing her chipped front tooth, she wore what Boehm called her bruised, sensuous look. The sunset colored her deep rose. Boehm drank from the bottle and kissed her, letting the mezcal flow from his mouth into hers. The slow kiss, mezcal dribbling down their chins, was like "two loving amoebas ingesting each other," he told Olivia.

"What an alarmingly rapacious image," she said, drawing back.

"For days," Boehm said, "I've felt as if a root boll were expanding in my head, bursting through my skull."

"*Please,* Steve," Olivia said. She trotted into the water.

In front of the thatched beachside restaurants the local children were raking the sand. They wore baggy white pants and T-shirts stamped in black letters SANEAMIENTO—sanitation —across the back, or no shirts at all. Floppy hats shadowed their faces. Listlessly they walked backward, dragging the rakes one-armed in straight paths that left as much trash as they gathered. The neat rows of bottles, wadded paper, squashed cups, and fruit rinds looked like a cultivated crop. The children scooped heaps of garbage in their arms and, without aiming, hurled the debris at a rusted oil drum, where it rattled down the outside and lay in a ring around the base.

"The place does have an odd feel this year," Boehm said to the man from Guadalajara.

"Yes, with only the children left behind."

"Where are the others?"

Las Playas had gone elsewhere to find work that summer, the man said. The oil accident—an American tanker bound for Long Beach—had destroyed most of the shrimp harvest in the spring. The fish catch was nonexistent. "And your tourism—I understand. Our inflation and your recession. The hotel people are unhappy. And now, of course, it's too hot for Americans." He clasped his hands and stretched, sighing.

One of the Guadalajara children was gravely offering Olivia his raft. Boehm watched as Olivia, not a swimmer, paddled laboriously in wide circles, straddling the raft with her slim, blonde legs.

Boehm sat up in the night, heart racing, the rush of adrenaline making him see weak white flashes in the dark. Beside him Olivia's breathing was deep and measured, the intervals between breaths interminably long. He pulled on his clothes and let himself into the hall. The hotel lobby was brightly lit. A tiny woman in an electric blue dress, elaborately coiffed hair rising a foot above her head and three artificial moles on her cheek, sat playing solitaire.

"Hey, tall-y. Tall man. Help me win."

As Boehm approached her she recrossed her legs and he saw she wasn't wearing underpants.

"Christ help me find the three of clubs," she said in a high, tinny voice.

Boehm stood behind her, looking at the cards. They were laid out in an unfamiliar pattern like the whorls of a shell.

"Lonely?" she said. Her upturned face was soft, unlined, the bones miniature. Boehm realized she was not yet a teenager.

"Come to my room," he said, not knowing why, except his heart had calmed, and the buzzing, burning sensation of his nerves had subsided. He led her down the hall. In the hotel room he switched on the dim lamp and drew down the sheet. Olivia lay on her stomach, one knee bent, cheek resting on her outstretched arm. Stray wisps of hair fluttered with her breath. Her body was amber and white.

"My wife," Boehm said. "Isn't she beautiful?"

The whore scratched her ear. She gave him a hard, direct look, devoid of shrewdness or coquetry. Boehm handed her a ten from his wallet.

"Good night," he said. He undressed and lay on the bed, listening to the lapping of the water.

The far wall glowed a hot, featureless white in the morning sun. Boehm didn't feel well rested. He came back from the bathroom and stood over Olivia's side of the bed.

She hadn't wanted the trip to Mexico. The reservations were months old and now the idea was grotesque, she had said, "a honeymoon for divorce." Finally she said she would do it for the guilt. Her affairs, Boehm interpreted. She claimed several, although at least one was bogus. The particular man had visited Boehm in Phoenix the night he supposedly spent with Olivia in San Francisco.

Already yesterday morning, their first, Boehm and Olivia had argued.

"*Pelicano*," she had said. "Look." The wheeling bird plummeted straight into the water, creating no perceptible splash, and disappeared except for the tips of its wings and tail. It bobbed up gulping a fish, crop quivering.

"*Pelicano*," Boehm said. "I never heard that cognate. I wonder if it's border Spanish."

"It's not border Spanish. It's the standard word."

"The word I learned was *alcatraz*."

"That's the prison," she said, "the island."

"It doesn't matter. They're probably both standard."

"Stand *up* for yourself, Steve. You think it's fairness but you're just being slippery." Abruptly she'd bundled her beach gear and returned to the hotel, where she'd read most of the day.

Boehm watched her sleep. "I feel like a buffalo tortured by mosquitoes," he whispered. "My head shaking, hooves pawing the dirt. Clouds of them. Their whine penetrates to every part of my body."

Boehm was a zookeeper, and had loved his animals, feeding and watering them, singing to them, snatching away the sugared junk thrown in their cages, bathing them. He had enjoyed watching the elephant shudder with pleasure under the hose. When unobserved he had tried to hug the animals, particularly those considered most aloof or dangerous. Though the animals nipped and kicked him, he had succeeded in hugging all but the carnivores. Some animals had injured themselves, struggling. Anticipating Olivia's absence, however, Boehm no longer cared about the animals. By the end of his shift, their cages, less well tended, would take on a tinge of rankness.

Boehm paraded naked before Olivia, daringly, knowing if she

woke she would think him fat. After her first affair he'd begun to eat very well, steaks, Belgian waffles, sundaes, fine liquor. He planted his heels with exaggerated firmness so that his bearded face quivered. Arms over his head he pirouetted, bourreed, feeling the jiggling of his thighs, chest, belly.

Olivia was obsessed with fresh vitamins, he reminded himself, and decided to buy her fruit for breakfast. The day before, a vendor had muscled his cart through the sand on the hour. Boehm put on his trunks and went down to the beach.

Low tide exposed brown blobs of rock. A veil of stranded seaweed, infested with flies, stretched to the highwater mark. The village children, *Los Saneamienteros,* as Boehm thought of them, were playing softball. They performed as if suffering from a neurological or muscular disorder. After an elaborate windup, the pitcher fell on his side during his delivery. Runners stumbled over the bases and veered into the outfield. Boehm moved closer, into the shadow of a thatched cabana. Without apparent cause, the first baseman toppled backward. A looping fly caromed off the third baseman's glove. He sank to his knees. Cursing, the pitcher charged him. The third baseman crawled after the ball, whirled, and flung it at the pitcher's head. It traveled slowly, like a balloon, struck the boy's cheek and fell to his feet. The pitcher's nose began to bleed.

The vendor's cart was stationed under an umbrella, surrounded by deserted beach. Boehm bought a slice of watermelon and sucked the seeds, falling into step several dozen paces behind the *saneamienteros,* who were wandering toward a row of *cantinas.* The two players still screamed at each other. Boehm heard footsteps just before Olivia reached him, snagging the waistband of his trunks with her finger. She wore her tiny flame orange bikini and her chest was flushed. She wanted to swim, she said, plucking at the elastic, touching his shoulder. Boehm realized his solitary walk had excited her. She loved him most, she had told him the first year of their marriage, when he was most absorbed in his own activity. Even simply rolling his sleeves could be enough.

Boehm took her hand and led her into the water. A hundred yards from shore Umichehueve reached only to Olivia's chin, Boehm's breastbone. Olivia ducked underwater and unfastened his drawstring. Boehm stripped off her suit, beloved by him, the anomaly in her wardrobe of soberly tailored slates, navies, tans. Olivia held his penis in both hands. Boehm hitched her legs around his waist. They kissed, rocking. Boehm felt himself exploring inside her. When he opened his eyes the blue of the sea and sky overwhelmed him. The color looked vast and granular. He was mesmerized by the white islands. He remembered a night when he'd lain over Olivia, feeling huge and gray, saying, this is all that matters to me, and she'd said, that's not really the idea, Steve. Now he moved her with his hands, held still while she moved herself, and she came, and again. Boehm couldn't come. This had never happened. He didn't think Olivia knew.

For the first time, Olivia agreed to go shopping in town. Holding her hand tightly in his very large one, Boehm escorted her along empty streets, always keeping between her and the curb, "an old custom, so the carriages don't splash mud on your finery, my dear." In fact, Olivia wore a plain white smock. Boehm's Mexican wedding shirt was embroidered with red and orange flowers, and the V-neck opened wide across his broad, curly-haired chest.

The air, shimmering with heat, looked like white smoke. A hot wind sent litter skipping across the pavement. Children sauntered past licking *paletas,* the glossy hues of tamarind, papaya, watermelon as vibrant as Polaroid. A *paleta* melted into a violet puddle on the sidewalk.

Most shops were closed. In a narrow wooden stand which filled the space between two department stores, Boehm bought

a scratchy, flamboyantly dyed hemp shopping bag ornamented
with straw butterflies.

"You big dingo, there's nothing to put in it," she said, laughing.
"There's nothing here."

"Just us."

"O.K., Steve," she said. She patted his hip and left her arm
wrapped around his waist. The shopping bag swung at her side.

They had bought only a few cans of tropical fruit nectar and a
half-liter of rum at the supermarket when they discovered Disco-
teca Saturday Night Fever. A simian, gyrating John Travolta was
painted on the stucco facade.

"Catch this," Boehm said. "A must, babe." The dance floor
was cramped and dark. A few children and young teenagers sat
against the wall. Cool air and music, "I Like the Night Life," one
of Boehm's favorites, blew from a vent in the ceiling. Boehm
loved disco. He hooked Olivia by the waist and swung her
around his head. She shrieked. Her smock flared out and settled
over his face as he lowered her.

Boehm had met Olivia when she was a student in the dance
class he taught for Parks and Recreation. She said he could see
any dance once, a samba, a minuet, a Balinese gamelan, and
perform it. He danced without needing to think.

"Dah-dah-dah-dah-DAH," Boehm sang between his teeth,
winding Olivia in, out, guiding her twirls with nudges from his
knee. He rocked her, draped her over his thigh, tossed her in
the air and caught her gently as the song ended.

The points of her cheeks were red. She rested her head on his
shoulder and bit his neck.

"Maybe we can go on after this," Boehm blurted.

She covered his mouth with her hand.

That night Boehm's whore was wearing an ostrich plume in
her hair and silver glitter around her eyes.

He would like some of her friends as well, Boehm said, the jangling of his nerves easing even as he spoke to her.

"They are all at the *Cantina Magui* smoking cigarettes and sitting on their *culos*. What they like is sitting on a man's cigarette and their *culos* smoking, ha ha."

He would wait in his room, Boehm said.

An hour later a procession of whores filed in, their fantastic hairdos casting shadows on the wall like the heads of mythical creatures. Boehm uncovered Olivia. He bent over her, held his hand a few inches over her face, and let it pass up and down her from head to ankle, without touching, as if stroking an invisible outer body.

"I like her legs best," Boehm said. His hands hovered over her thighs, then dragged toward her feet as if encountering resistance from the flesh.

"Now you do it," he said to the girl with the ostrich feather.

"She'll wake up and yell."

"No she won't." He took the girl's hand and skimmed it along the warmth that blanketed Olivia's body like an atmosphere. He stood back. Palms outstretched, the whore's hands made sweeping flights over Olivia. Her arms followed the motion, then her torso, until she was swaying rhythmically. She began to hum softly, almost in a whisper. Boehm gestured to the others. They surrounded the bed, heads inclined. Their hands made small circles over Olivia, then moved out from her center and down her sides, as if molding a sand angel. The paths of their hands crossed, weaving over and under each other. The whores hummed.

Olivia's breathing deepened. The gaudily enameled fingernails seemed to be spinning a cocoon around her.

"Touch," Boehm said. A border of sixty fingers radiated, like fluting, from Olivia. She looked like a profane Lady of Guadalupe.

Olivia flinched and groaned. The whores' hands recoiled. Olivia curled into a ball, hand clenching and opening, fingers spread wide. Boehm flipped off the lightswitch and lay beside her. She groaned again, and rolling onto her other side, slapped her arm against Boehm's chest.

"It's hot," she said. "It feels strange. You're all dressed up." Boehm heard her respiration, thick against the sheet, become slow and even. The breathing of the whores was like seafoam hissing around a stone.

Boehm paid the whores in the hall. None of them, he saw, could have been older than twelve. When they turned the corner toward the lobby they broke into frenzied giggling.

The next morning Olivia complained of feeling weak, with an upset stomach. Boehm suggested they stroll to an inlet where the town children played, and get their fresh air before the day's heat. The inlet was marked by a jetty, an outcropping of black volcanic boulders like an immense dorsal fin rising from the water. To Boehm's right sat the row of peeling *cantinas*. Directly ahead, a circle of Mexicans, mostly children, had gathered on the beach. Women in the local bathing uniform of shorts and baggy blouses were clapping their hands, laughing. Arms folded across their chests, men drank beer, smiling sternly.

"Barbecue," Boehm said.

Then he saw the rakes rising and falling quickly like threshing rods, and the pelican, foolishly tilted head and broken wings, lurching toward the edge of the circle, fluttering under the blows of the *saneamienteros*.

"What are you doing?" Olivia cried, running into the midst of the circle. One of the *saneamienteros* struck the pelican in the middle of its long neck. The bird's head flopped to the sand. Olivia screamed at them. Boehm charged the boys, fists clenched, stopped, pumped his arms, relaxed. A spectator shrugged. Others shook their heads. There was laughter, and the people moved away. The *saneamienteros* slipped their sticks under the dead bird and tossed it into the air. Olivia sprawled on the sand, crying.

"I hate Mexico," she said when Boehm reached her. "Why do I have to go through this? I want to go home, today."

They couldn't get to the station in time for the day's train, Boehm said.

"Tomorrow. I'm leaving tomorrow."

All right, Boehm said. For now she should lie down in their room.

"I don't want to go back there."

The gazebo, Boehm suggested. Olivia had wanted to visit the bronze-roofed landmark, built when the hotel was Porfirio Diaz's personal resort.

"Why didn't you do something about that bird? How could you stand there? Think of your animals, Steve."

"It's their way. This is another culture," Boehm murmured. His comprehension filled him with serenity. "Animals shrink to nothing in a landscape like this," he said dreamily. "It would take herds and herds of them, thousands, to matter." Boehm thought of his zoo enclosures and couldn't visualize animals inside them. The iron cages, their contours of sandstone-colored gunnite, were empty.

Olivia stared at him. "Poor Steve," she said.

"But I feel like that bird."

Olivia wouldn't respond.

The stretch of beach to the gazebo's rocky hill was white and blank. Its terraced gardens were overgrown with weeds. Livid green grass sprouted between the tiles of the walkway.

"So this is our last night," Boehm said. Olivia wouldn't look at him. "Olivia," Boehm said, voice cracking, "this is our last night." He squeezed her arm.

"Don't." She shrugged away. In the gazebo two stone benches were set in an L, not quite joining. Olivia lay on one, feet toward the water. Boehm lowered himself onto the other. The stone surface was cool under his back. A hot wind ruffled his sleeves. Boehm could see the beaches falling away down the coast. He understood a fever was coming on, and then he was asleep.

When they woke, both were sluggish with fever. Hand in hand, without speaking, they walked back along the glittering beach. While they sipped fruit nectars laced with rum on the hotel veranda, the Guadalajara man joined them, drinking mineral water.

"There was a shark this morning." The man nodded toward the bay. "Be careful. I had lunch with the director of tourism and he said it was a porpoise. Flipper." He laughed. "I asked him to accompany me for a swim then, but he said he had important conferences."

"The children killed a pelican this morning," Olivia said. She told the story, crying again.

The man's brow furrowed. "The people's lives are horrible. They have become ugly. I'm sorry. It wasn't always this way."

Boehm and Olivia finished their drinks. The sugared alcohol seemed to make the sickness burn through Boehm's body. His brain felt bloated and clogged.

"I need to lie down," Olivia said. "I feel like I'm going to faint. Thank you," she said to the Guadalajara man. She clasped his wrist. If she'd stayed the full week, Boehm thought, she and the man would have become lovers.

In their room Boehm and Olivia made love for a long time. Afterwards Boehm stayed inside her, dozing. Then he rolled away. Olivia curled against him, rubbing her face against his chest, his face, crying.

When they were first married, she told him, she would speed to the zoo on her lunch hour and spy on him. The unfamiliarity of his uniform—white shirt, gray slacks—and of his stately pace from cage to cage frightened and thrilled her. "But then that day I poked you in the ribs and you spun around and dropped the feed bag. You pranced, and imitated the animals, and draped your arm around me, giving me your weight in that way you have, and kiss kiss kiss. You were exactly the same. I was so disappointed! I'm sorry." Her voice was hoarse. "I feel so bad. I knew two years ago but I couldn't admit it. It's my fault."

Boehm woke remembering a cocktail party at their home. Gracious but withdrawn, Olivia poured drinks—bare arms against the glass tabletop—and watered the chrysanthemums. The wind molded the white muslin dress to her body, giving her the appearance of rough plaster sculpture. After the guests left, she and Boehm danced on the lawn. He lifted the dress over her head.

"Wait," she said, catching his wrist. "Stand beside me. Hold my hand. Can't you ever be content just like this?"

The patio spotlight made her skin glisten as if wet. Shaking his head miserably, Boehm slipped her underpants down her thighs. How could he tell her he wanted to wear her skin over his, that he desired her body so much he wished it to be his own, to feel himself enter her?

In bed next to Boehm, Olivia tossed, sweating, yet after a double dose of the medication her breathing, though harsh, was regular and incredibly slow. Boehm dressed. The hotel lobby was empty. Feeling the electricity in his veins, he clattered down the wooden stairs to the beach and started for the *cantinas*. In the moonlight the sky and water were sludge gray.

The *Cantina Magui* was lit by lavender tubes at either side of the jukebox. The ceiling was black, the frayed carpeting crimson. Dark red plastic roses were pinned to the walls. A nude blonde woman in an Uncle Sam top hat danced obscenely on stage.

Boehm took a booth. Jammed into a booth opposite, the whores chattered with nervously animated gestures. They didn't acknowledge him. A tall waiter with a sad face and drooping gray mustache served him. When the waiter turned away, Boehm saw a long slash in his trouser leg. The *saneamienteros,* occupying the tables nearest the stage, threw wadded napkins and lime twists at the dancer. Laughing, she kicked the debris back in their faces. A lighted butt struck her thigh with a shower of sparks. She winced, swearing.

The atmosphere lulled Boehm. He sipped his drink and stretched out his long legs. He waved at the whores but still they paid him no attention. He didn't know what he wanted with them. He drummed his fingers on the table and sang a little song. He went to the *saneamienteros'* tables.

"Birdman." They laughed. "And where is Mrs. Birdman this night?" A boy made a clacking pelican bill with his hands in front of his mouth. "Always shouting."

The children crowded around him, jostling, their eyes murky and glazed. Boehm imagined himself sinking to the floor under their rhythmic blows. The image momentarily appealed to him, but he said, "I have beer money at my hotel. Come back and party."

"Hey. O.K." The boys whistled for the whores. "Ladies."

The scuffing of small feet followed Boehm to the hotel. Leaving the children outside his door, he went to the hotel bar. In his room, he flicked the light switch with his arm and set a case of Carta Blanca on the dresser. Olivia writhed from side to side under the sheet, frowning, lip curled over her chipped tooth. Spirals of hair clung to her face. The bed was soaked.

Sitting cross-legged on the floor, the whores passed beer and lit each other's cigarettes with silver lighters, fanning smoke away from their faces. The boys scrabbled through luggage and drawers, bickering over valuables, jerking the bottles to their lips. Beer foamed out of their mouths.

"Now I'm going to show you about love," Boehm said. He braced Olivia's shoulders and sat her upright. Her skin was washed with sweat. He caressed her hair, twining the strands

around his fingers. In the wall mirror he glimpsed his disembodied hands at her head. He remembered the child's game: the
performer crosses arms and fondles the back of his own head,
neck, shoulders, his hands appearing to be those of a hidden
lover. Boehm felt as if he were vanishing, becoming Olivia's
hands. Olivia sat alone on the bed, making love to herself.

Boehm jumped as if shocked. Trembling, nerves stinging, he
kissed her. Her mouth was slack. He kissed her again, smacking
his own lips resoundingly to imitate the noise of two people
kissing. Her head lolled against his shoulder. Repeatedly, loudly,
he kissed her.

"All right, sleep then. Sure, O.K., just go right ahead, sleeping. Christ." Boehm shook out capsules and forced them down
Olivia's throat, pouring beer after. Olivia gulped convulsively,
opened her eyes. Wide and alert, they met Boehm's in a level
gaze, then squinted shut. She whipped her head back and forth,
quieted, sighing. Her chin dropped to her breast.

"She can't be in here," Boehm said. He lifted Olivia in his
arms. The sheet crumpled to one side. Passing the Guadalajara
man's door, he shushed the children in an undertone. Outdoors,
a warm wind beat against their faces. Strips of cloud slid across
the moon. At a sand hillock midway between the water and the
cabanas, Boehm told the children, "Dig here."

The *saneamienteros* scooped the sand easily. Moonlight turned
Olivia's pubic hair silver, bleached buildings and palm trees so
that they had no depth. Far out to sea, a green shine lay on
the water.

It seemed that Olivia had stopped breathing. Boehm covered
her mouth with his and blew air into her lungs. Her chest ex-
panded, deflated. Frantically he drew air, released it into her,
over and over. Her chest rose and fell with his rhythm. Even after
her breath caught raggedly, held, Boehm continued to breathe
with her. Breathing for her, his body was soothed and refreshed.
He felt the beginnings of happiness.

He laid her in the hole, knees tucked against her chest, and buried her to the neck. Her head tilted to one side. Her breathing cracked the crust of sand over her chest. Stooping, Boehm brushed grains from her eyelids and cheek. The children were skipping and singing, and, linking arms with a boy and girl, Boehm joined them, feeling light as a ghost. He started toward the hotel to pack his belongings.

The green radiance, riding swells toward land, had filled the bay. Plankton, Boehm knew, billions of phosphorescent organisms. Light rose from the water like a miasma, a virulent green fog.

The first green wave poised to strike the beach.

THE BIG BANG AND THE GOOD HOUSE

The morning is thick enough to stir with a spoon. The tower of waffle is cold in a puddle of congealed syrup, sweet and good. My wife Annie's nightgown is open to a beauty mark on her collarbone, which she taps distractedly with a pencil. Replying to her students' journals occupies hours of her weekend.

"Look here," I say. "They think the universe might have arisen out of pure nothing." From the newspaper I read:

> Even the void has mathematical structure. If that structure, that "nothing," becomes unstable, through a random quantum event . . .

"Presto," I say. "Instant universe. The Big Bang." A jagged hole ripped in the fabric of things, and the black nothing rushing outward.

The objects in our kitchen, even my bathrobe, seem to stir. My scalp prickles. Senses keen with panic or desire, I smell the bready morning scent of Annie's body. Grabbing her hand, I lead her toward the bedroom, but as we undress my urgency goes and I must flog myself through it. This has been happening.

Annie smoothes my forehead. "Tony, it's time we had a child."

"All right." It's as simple as that.

The next morning I take refuge with a riprapping crew, heaving boulders, rather than presiding over DesertScapes, my nursery.

DesertScapes' profit is hemorrhage in reverse, no use to anyone, not Annie, with her respectable teacher's salary and modest tastes. The trim nape of her neck is a statement of self-sufficiency. Recently I aired TV commercials exposing the disadvantages of my product. A beach ball deflated on an agave tip. Tweezers plucked millions of prickly pear barbs from panty hose. Mesquite branch snagged toupee. For the finale I sat on a barrel cactus, delivered an urbane pitch, then struggled vainly to rise. Sales ballooned another 19 percent.

At the end of my workday, I tuck an ocotillo in the pickup bed for a fertility planting ritual. Delighted, Annie buries her diaphragm in the winter socks drawer. We've disagreed over the yard. When we bought the house, it was scoured bare, and I've chosen to leave it that way. In dry, monochrome June the vacant plain seethes as if it might crack.

We choose a site by the kitchen window. I pick through caliche, Annie shovels dirt. Her happiness elates me. The sun is marvelously hot, and sweat bursts from us, streaming down Annie's spine. I tongue it off, lifting her shirt. She bites my shoulder. Before setting the root boll we pop a beer, trade sips, and pour the can into the hole. I imagine ocotillo seeds littering the ground. Ocotillo thickets choke the yard; a sea of tossing red blossoms swallows the house.

Though our next stop is bed, I'm not in the mood, definitely. "It's good just to be held," Annie says.

"Goal-directed impotence. A vintage 80's concept," I say.

Memorial Day we're driving the interstate to Annie's family, the Herreras. The hundred miles between our cities glide by like water, as if we're paddling lazily, hands trailing in the river. This contentment when visiting the Herreras, which overrides whatever else we might be feeling, is the great achievement of our marriage. Three years' worth.

When I met Annie, she'd renounced her father over his infidelity. Because I'm true, she explains, the adultery no longer exists.

"Healed?" I suggest.

"Never happened. He didn't cheat. You've replaced that. It's a kind of transubstantiation. You'd have to be Catholic."

Annie nestled in my arm, the music on the oldies station sounds big. For the first time I feel joy about the baby plan. I know it will work.

When we arrive, the Herreras are frisky about our "trying."

"Nothing good was ever accomplished without honest effort. Unnh," Mr. Herrera grunts, winking. When he's out of earshot, Annie's mother confides naturopathic advice, spices to avoid, herbs to apply. These she smuggles to Annie in Baggies.

A barbecue at the Herreras is no humble matter of hibachi and charcoal. Consistent with the estate's Grecian theme—the mansion is a full-scale replica of the Parthenon—three marble torches, fueled by subterranean gas rivers, spew flame. Around them white-clad kitchen servants undulate hieratically, plunging long-handled forks into the spitting meat.

Just before serving, Mr. Herrera takes Annie's hands in one of his, mine in the other. The family stands around us, smiling faces roasted in the late afternoon light. All bow our heads. "Bless your child," Mr. Herrera says. Shivering, I clench his hand.

Driving home, over a hundred miles, Annie has dropped off, head against the seat rest. We are enclosed by the dark, our knees, lit by the dash bulb, reflected inside the windshield. Those bright, isolated smudges, her left knee and my right, are so dear to me my throat tightens. Resenting even the cone of road, yellow dotted line, illuminated ahead, I cut the headlights.

With no moon I see nothing. I can't even be sure we're moving. The hair rises on my neck. The wind rushes by, not as sound but as the blackness touching my face. My foot presses to the floor. The car begins vibrating. The dark is irresistibly beautiful. My eyes are wet. Though my foot cramps fighting to release the gas pedal, I can't let go the blackness, my body shaking, its paralysis, the tears rolling. Any moment Annie's voice will break in—wake up!

But instead there's weightlessness, jarring, rocks spattering the chassis. Annie yells once, I punch on the lights. We are sliding broadside in a wide arc. Creosote and palo verde blur past, clubbing the hood. The oncoming hillside tilts suddenly as we are upended over a wash. We crawl up and out my door, drop to the ground. The car crunches into the gulley, spraying glass. The beams light clusters of foliage.

An immediate, photographic recollection comes to me. While we slump in the back of a Highway Patrol cruiser, drained calm, I ask, "Do you remember the shoebox house?"

"Of course. I'd never forget. Doesn't it seem like another life?"

"Oh, man. Have you got it wrong." I shake my head. This is the other life.

When I was busted, five years ago, I was twenty-two. Selling but mostly consuming narcotics and psychedelics, I conducted business through a weird tumbling of states, coke's gregarious high-stepping giving way to the austere spaciousness, then private riot, of acid.

Like hell, prison always had seemed a punitive societal myth, metaphorically purifying the spirit without one's actually having to go there. Since the other cons were hallucinations, I didn't speak to them. I performed my duty in the yard, picking trash that was replaced in the same location the next day. Refusing to join any faction in the gang wars, I catalyzed more violence—

fists, feet, a tin shank, mop wringer handle, blood draining in the shower stall. I slashed at people without feeling anything about them. With as little reason they slugged my kidneys.

Spurts of anxiety flushed away my substance, leaving me dainty, transparent. Looking through myself, I saw the ground behind, pebbles casting miniscule noontime shadows.

For the general security and my own safety, I was isolated in the Hole, a windowless cell with cement bed. Nights were devoid of light, an emptiness that jumped, chattered, far more energetic than I. It was absorbing me. I didn't know where I began or ended, what was inner or outer. Rising from the bed, I believed my legs were left behind, and my thighs tensed as if still sitting. It was bland agony, like attending a party, mechanically smiling, and shaking hands while under my dress suit the adhesive tissue between skin and muscle was being cut, the skin slipped off.

Other times I was mildly euphoric, lying on the bed, strands of myself spooling into the cosmos, pulled by tides of space. It was in this mood that I slid apart the halves of a doctored shirt button, extracted a quarter-inch razor blade, and opened my wrists. The invisible blood dripped loudly.

The guard's periodic check was in time. Transferred to the state psychiatric hospital, I awaited the investigation that would officially commit me. Abruptly, the chronic jostling for space at a public institution forced my discharge. Supplied with parole officer, therapist, prescription, and a few bucks, I was put on a bus. By the time I reached my stop a cool storm muffled the city. I ducked into the first bar, the E-Z Lounge.

The stools were soft red plastic, rips taped.

"You look bandaged," the barmaid said. "Take off your cap."

Shift's end, I bought her a drink.

"Annie Herrera," she introduced herself, sitting beside me. She looked like someone inadequately disguised. A ducktail frayed over her collar as she threw back her head, chugging a cigarette. Her breasts wobbled inside a baggy T-shirt. Yet her face was symmetrical and lucid as a shell.

"I ran away from home," she said, that being her father's Parthenon overlooking the state capital. Every evening he climbed an adjacent hill to admire the last sun gilding the portico. "He's a pathetic blowfish," Annie said. "Now I rent a shoebox for $110 a month."

She drank quickly. A ceiling bulb pulsed behind her head. With her incomplete loveliness entrancing me, her descriptions took on the force of image—roaches like bronze buttons rolling loose across her floor, her father's lonely vigil on the mountain, his friends flopping like slugs into the jacuzzi.

"I could have married a congressman," she said. "His stomach hung over his tiny bathing suit. If he was naked, it would have covered his penis." Neighboring drinkers glanced at her. "Penis," she repeated loudly. A man shouldered beside her, ordering. Her elbow jerked as if he had snotted it, or ejaculated on it.

I kept imagining she was dropping something, and I was picking it up for her. I wished it would happen. Then she would keep talking.

"You listen," she said. "Men don't listen. If you say what they expect, they explain it for you. If you say something interesting, they deny it. What do you do?"

"I washed out of prison." I told what I considered a funny story about my original cellmates. The popeyed kid had constructed a woman from a pillow and a sheet stuffed with his clothes. Every night Pop humped her until the wide-shouldered, pompadoured lover of the unit could stand no more. While Pop was on the crapper, Pompadour stole her for himself.

Tears came to Annie's eyes. "That's a terrible story," she said, taking my hands in hers. "I liked you since you came in."

Every hair, my prick, stood on end, straining toward her. I kissed her mouth.

"I don't come," she crooned in my ear, as if it were the most lascivious suggestion imaginable.

We made love all our first twenty-four hours in the shoebox house. Through thin blue curtains sunlight drenched the bed, built into an alcove, and there we were, somebody's butt in the air, somebody's face buried in someone else's neck. Finally Annie was distinct, sitting beside me, untangling her hair with a stiff brush.

I had no background, I said. My history began with her. I lived in the sensations of my hands slippery over her body, the musk of her armpit and groin, her breast shaped to my mouth.

"I'd do anything to make you come," I said.

"Lick my asshole?"

It was salty as the rest of her.

"Lock yourself in the closet and stay there all day?"

I took the key in with me and turned it. The light sucked out, I sat in the exploding and collapsing densities, palms wet, breath tight.

"Please come out. I'm going to call the fire department." She beat the door. "The kettle's boiling. If you're not out by the time I count a hundred, I'm going to pour it on my arm."

"No you won't," I yelled back, and she burst into sobs.

The radio came on top volume, then the vacuum cleaner.

About noon I came out. The house was immaculate. Paper towels folded into birds spilled from the glasses on the table. "Easy," Annie said. "This is how the maids do it at home. But I'm not ready. Go back in." She laughed, silver hoop earrings dangling. The line of her cheekbones was so clean I could feel a coolness around her head.

She served caviar on a filagreed silver dish, relic of her family's Mexico City origins; chilled wine; her one consistent success, poached fish.

"It's not enough," she said.

A few days later Annie said, "I think I feel something," and she came. "Oh," she kept saying, tossing her head, eyes closed. Side by side we lay in the sopping bedclothes. Only her finger moved, tracing my entire body as if coloring me in.

Her hands closed on my wrist as if it were my throat. "You can never leave me now," she said, and then, "Don't ever bring another woman inside me."

I think we might have enjoyed some repose then, but for my recurring panics. As I walked toward the Circle K one morning, something was wrong with the chinaberry trees. They became flat and stringy, then faded altogether. I felt the familiar bloating lightness. What if I fell in the street? A car skidding the corner . . .

"You can't go out until you're well," Annie said. "Don't worry about work." She took an extra shift.

Alone at night, fear made me sick. I began accompanying Annie to the bar, where I nursed a beer, chatted with the manager, shot pool. At the bar a drunk reached for her breast; I caught his wrist and smashed his fingers on the counter. "Oh, Jesus," Annie said, hands shaking. Carrying an armload of glasses, she slipped on the rubber mat. Her ankle, twisting beneath her, broke.

Because she was employed on the sly, Annie couldn't claim disability. My assets had been seized by the IRS. Our money ran out. Though I hadn't left home alone in six weeks, I found a yard job in the classifieds. Annie swung alongside on stork-leg crutches to see me off. I was so frightened that my gas pedal foot and my hands seemed disembodied, floating beside me. But I backed out the drive. For hoeing and burning weeds I was paid cash.

Gradually potted cacti and desert shrubs accumulated in our backyard. Cheap or less, hauled from development sites, they enabled me to bid more ambitious jobs. Customers were pleased with my gravel lawns, rock and mortar whodunits, oddments of brick and railroad tie, accented with plants. Income-producing thought issued like jet vapor from my head. With the Sun Belt boom, overpopulation had driven up water rates, and the desert was chic. By mid-fall I'd bought a monstrous old V-8 pickup and formed a crew.

Healed, Annie didn't return to the bar. Perennially employable, she took and quit jobs with an auto parts distributor, real estate office, Shaklee. Typically she drank rum-and-Coke and snoozed away the afternoon.

"You're making three hundred a week. Why should I work at all?" she said spitefully.

Why indeed? I said.

"At your jobs the women spy through the blinds when you take your shirt off," she said.

"They don't tell me about it."

Without the need to care for me, or earn, Annie buzzed with her own discontents. Increasingly, they centered on Mexico.

The Fall of the Herreras had occurred when Annie's grandfather, a federal minister in post–World War II Mexico City, was ousted by scandal, the family holdings confiscated. "It was jealousy, you can bet," Annie said. "Too popular, worshipped by the poor, the old story." He'd lived another twenty years, selling shoes in Leon.

His son, Annie's father, had smuggled her family across the border. They lived under a bridge. Annie's first memory was of clutching a junked sofa leg as the river swept away their living room. Now the Herreras were forbidden to mention that time, or even to speak Spanish. Her father, owner of a resort, was more American than Johnny Carson, Annie said.

"He betrays his kind," she said, shrugging. When two years earlier he had confessed the affair, his wife had a stroke. "You should have seen Mama." Annie's head slewed limply.

I suggested Annie take Spanish. Spring semester she enrolled in Level I at the community college. Our belongings acquired neatly typed labels—*la silla, el espejo, el refrigerador*—as if our house had sprouted yellow leaves. She called herself Ana.

She bought a flowered Mexican clothes hook in the border town. Bark tapestries unrolled down our walls, we drank water from hand-blown Tlaquepaque glass. Annie let her hair grow out curly, fastening it with Taxco silver combs. Our tostadas and enchiladas suizas were bathed in homemade salsa. Annie ate intently, guacamole overflowing the tortilla onto her fingers. She gained weight in her hips, belly, and chin. Then twenty-two pounds crashed in a water-only diet.

Jumping a semester to intermediate, she continued Spanish in summer school and volunteered at a clinic for illegal aliens.

In July an invitation to the Herreras' twenty-fifth anniversary provoked our first serious fight.

"I've never met them," I insisted.

"It would humiliate me for you to see him."

"I'll go by myself."

Annie's arms shot out and the table went over. "I can't do that to them." She fell into a chair.

I'd never liked my family either, I said, soothing her. Forever nicking himself, my father applied Band-Aids that perfectly matched his skin; he was the only flesh-colored person I've known. My mother applied herself to perkiness and crossword puzzles. Both brothers quit school for the service; my sister eloped at sixteen.

Mr. Herrera was sleek and compact, hair still black, but with silver handlebar mustaches. His silk shirt was the violent primary colors of jujubes, open over his hairless chest. He had that edge of embittered self-congratulation typical of showbiz personalities—"My Way," "Made It Through the Rain." But he could begin a story "At our anniversary fete last night the Governor contributed a fountain of Dom Perignon ten feet high" and end "This morning already I'm unfaithful. For two hours I embraced the toilet bowl, kissing the seat."

"Is he bluffing?" Annie hissed in my ear. "Does he think we don't know?" Mrs. Herrera's mouth still drooped at the corner, vestige of the stroke.

Handing me a drink, Mr. Herrera propelled me up the lookout mountain, which he also owned. As we seated ourselves on a cement bench carved with Winged Victories, colored beams whipped across the Parthenon's Doric columns.

"Self-activates at dusk," Mr. Herrera said. "And a hell of a security system, too. Criminals think they've died and gone to heaven up here. Annie tells me you're a businessman."

I deprecated my backyard nursery.

"Where do you think everyone begins? Look, I must tell you, you're not the first man for Annie, because such are these times. She has made unfortunate attachments. But she is a constant girl. Months go by, she sees no one if a man is unsuitable. So already I'm impressed with you."

After dinner, as the manservant cleared the table, Annie complimented the meal in Spanish. Nobody responded.

"*Verdad, Ana, y el vino también,*" I said finally.

"Americans speak English," Mr. Herrera said.

"Yes," Annie said, "you and Ronald Reagan, you and La Migra, you and the CIA in Nicaragua, you and the Justice Department that sends refugees, Latinos like yourself, home to be killed."

Mr. Herrera reddened. Two of Annie's sisters, on the far end of the marble dining hall, elaborately flung their napkins onto the floor. "Leave this table," Mrs. Herrera said.

As Annie snatched up her shawl, Mr. Herrera attempted a wink in my direction, but he was so agitated that his eyelid wouldn't close. He looked as if lemon had squirted his eye. "Wait," he whispered, commanding with a strong hand on my arm. "If you were my son-in-law, I would have a family stake investing in your business. You need capital to expand. What are you going to do, put up a circus tent in your backyard?" Smiling with astonishment, I waved around the table and followed Annie to the car, where she sat with chin jutted.

"Of course he's despicable," I said. "But he loves you so much he's in danger. You have the power to shame his life away." A surprising love for him tugged at me. Like me he was made over, too new, scrubbed pink like surgically reconstructed skin.

"If I found my grandfather's house in Mexico City," Annie was saying, "I would creep on my knees like pilgrims at the Basilica. I'd photograph every square foot and make postcards, and send one to my father each day saying, 'This is your home.'"

At the end of summer school we crossed the border to recover Annie's grandfather, at least his reputation. The violation of my parole gave us both insomnia. Mexico City was a Hollywood disaster movie, a postnuclear epic. In a pall of charred smog we traipsed from government agency to library to newspaper archive. Her grandfather, we learned, had been purged as a Nazi collaborator. The ancestral Herrera home was located in the suburb Pedregal de San Angel, an enclave of multimillion-dollar villas surrounded by massive lava walls. Shanties leaned against them. Old women bent double under loads of bound sticks. Babies slept in boxes. Within, the current occupants toasted us with cocktails and stuffed us with hors d'oeuvres.

Outside, Annie burst into sobs as I held her. Then, shaking free, she raised her arms, slowly, high overhead, and let them slap to her sides.

On the train north she was composed, seductive, peeling fresh mango and popping it in my mouth. Home, she registered at the university. Within two years she had completed an abandoned degree program, student teaching, and certification. She was assigned a fourth grade.

We married. Negotiations surrounded the ceremony. I had not entered a church in a decade and a half, but Mrs. Herrera wanted a religious service; a priest married us in our backyard. Annie demanded a Mexican extravaganza reception. The priest, in a white linen cassock, rope-belted, seemed as alien as a guest lead from *Star Trek*. He was middle-aged handsome, with sharp chin and graying hair, and surprised me with a whistle when Annie and I kissed, closing our vows. It was a beautiful September day, breezes rippling the shadows of leaves over us.

For the reception, the rented ballroom was decked with streamers and paper flowers. While mariachis played on stage, Annie and I drank champagne from the bottle. The dancing began, *el Baile del Dolar*. Mr. Herrera first partnered Annie, who, pliant as a shop dummy, looked woodenly past him. My own family not attending, I engaged Mrs. Herrera, Celia, instead of my mother. Though hippy, she was an effortless bundle, strands of her gray hair flying across my face. At the song's conclusion she knotted a C-note in my bowtie. The next partner, an aunt, tucked a more modest five into my belt. The band repeated "Volver Volver," dance after dance.

Sprigs of legal tender wound into my hair, protruding from my shoes, pinned into a tail behind me, I blundered into Annie and Mrs. Herrera huddling against the stage.

"I have forgiven him," Mrs. Herrera was saying, forefinger punching her own chest. "How is it your business to go on punishing him?" I drifted away in the arms of a perfumed fourteen-year-old cousin.

And so Mr. Herrera promenaded Annie into the center again, he nimble on small feet, she festooned with gray-green currency bows. His cheeks were split wide with smiling. The last trumpet quaver, she patted his shoulder and kissed his cheek, stood while he hugged her.

True to his word, Mr. Herrera presented me with a choice parcel of B-2, now DesertScapes. Annie and I bought a house.

At her request Annie was transferred to a barrio school. Nightly she treated me to the latest marvels of border Spanglish: "*Oye, K-mart tiene el gran half-price sale de Voltron y los Gobots, esta noche hasta los diez, check it out . . .* " She bought me season basketball tickets and rubbed linament in my joints, stretched my back and neck. Her facial angularity subsided, lines rounding. Even her movements softened. She settled into furniture like a release of air.

My parole expired. I discontinued therapy. We were complete, my job finished.

Annie's version of the Memorial Day crash: "We hit so hard it knocked the lights out for a second." The car is totalled, crushed.

In a dream I take my child to the junkies' restaurant.

"Coming along great, Tony," the waiter fawns. He, like all the employees and clientele, like me, is unremarkable except for the left arm, shrunken and chalky. In the dream it's understood this is the mainlining arm (though I never have shot dope and indeed will not take even aspirin now). The baby is healthy-sized except for its left arm, also withered.

Recoiling from myself, I recede faster from Annie. Weeks pass without a caress, much less sex.

"O.K.," Annie says. "I will take the diaphragm out of the drawer. I will put it in."

I wave her off.

Summer, and women approach DesertScapes uncovered. Triangular cloth bits hold in their breasts. Their cutoffs ride low on the hips, frayed denim crotches scarcely wider than the perineum. Their apricot-gold flesh circulates, liquid, among islands of stark, grotesque desert forms. Today a woman's pinky nail traces for me the color modulations in one prickly pear pad.

Casually her hand loops the needles. My finger wants to follow the line of her crouched thigh and calf. Her fluffy blonde hair is pinned behind her ear. I even half-step toward her, then kneel quickly, tying my shoe. She is maybe nineteen.

Her next visit she asks if I truly sat on the barrel cactus, on TV.

"For reals. No special effects at DesertScapes," I say.

She winces. "I have to tell you, I find the whole series kind of contemptuous toward the plants," she says.

"Flippancy is just the surface of despair."

"For what?"

"I don't know why I said that. It must be your naked ear."

In the greenhouse where I keep my rarest exotics, I pull her to me by the small of her back. Her arms band around me. I reach inside her cutoffs and flow into her through my hands. I become her dry, compact buttocks, long nipples stabbing my chest, legs pressed against me. A groan reverberates through me.

"I can't be doing this," I say. "My wife and I are making a baby."

"All right." She steps back lightly, shedding the experience. "Good luck."

But she, Lou, returns. "What a nice sunburned man," she says when we undress in her apartment. There is nothing we will not do for each other. During what I tell Annie is a procuring trip to Baja California, I don't leave Lou's apartment for seventy-two hours. Finally, after days of coupling, a fantasm of ourselves separates from us. Bluish, it hovers and bumps along the ceiling, pure dim light like those fish at the ocean bottom.

Annie changes her hairstyle, a flip, a perm. She wears peekaboo negligees to bed and brings home X-rated videos. I find a push-up bra in the laundry, though she is full-breasted. She buys a health spa membership.

"What is it?" she says. She is discernible but hard to identify, as if we're looking at each other through the windows of parallel trains traveling at high speed.

I agree to resume with my therapist, but I don't keep the appointments. Annie summons Mr. Herrera, whose latest hobby, a helicopter, lands in our backyard, blades thundering, winds blasting choking storms of dust.

"It's not so bad, having a child," he says, as we sip beers against the carport. "They only cut their heads open, break their hearts, kill themselves with drugs and grow up to hate you. Why worry?"

But I'm not smiling. His image suffers from the same opacity as his daughter's.

"Isn't she pretty to you any more?"

"It's not that, Mike."

Lowering his voice, though Annie is inside, he says, "Distractions can occur." His eyes shift. We haven't acknowledged his infidelity.

"There's no big deal," I say. "Some kind of phase. It'll pass."

Though Annie and I see each other daily, her face is a spent bulb. Daily workouts have given her the kite-shaped torso of a weightlifter. Her back is rows of glowering muscle.

The phone wakes Annie and me late at night. I grope for it, say hello. No one speaks, a half minute, more.

The light flashes on. Annie's face is pale, grim.

Arching my eyebrows, I hand her the receiver, my stomach knotting, heart pounding. But for her it's the same. Silence funnels into the room.

Annie's expression wavers, her mouth relaxing while the frown deepens. Her glance flicks at me, hides.

Over the next days she alternates between flat hostility and remorseful tenderness.

Lou explains the phone call. "I wanted to hear where you live. Another way of making love."

Lou and I invent Hot Massage, holding our palms over a candle flame until the heat sears, then pressing quickly into each other's flesh. A rubber band around the scrotum, we discover, delays climax for hours. I ejaculate blood spots. When the topic turns to snuff films we fall silent, contemplating the image of our joined bodies, golden in cheap incandescent light, jolted, rising slow motion out of the frame.

Shopping, we guide our cart among customers pinched or rushed or dreamily intent, who give us no particular attention. Parking against the freezer, selecting orange juice, black-eyed peas, we could be a couple like any other, in another supermarket, in another life. Home, we smear each other's bodies into paste.

Edging onto Broadway from Lou's street, I see Annie's Nissan and merge two cars behind. Stopped in a rush-hour jam, she glances compulsively in the rearview mirror, fussing at her eyebrows, and I'm certain she'll notice me in the elevated pickup cab. Her head nods, and I identify the new sound as Top 40, then a Mexican ballad, jazz, classical, country. Nothing fits—I know the feeling. I tense for her. The light changing, she taps her horn repeatedly.

She pulls off at the health club, and I park around the corner, delaying before I enter. Through the steamy partition between sauna and Nautilus I watch her legs scissoring, a delicate winglike bar dipping behind her shoulders. The violent effort compresses her face.

At the convenience mart she buys milk and cartons I can't identify from the lot across the street. It's getting dark.

Her final stop is the drugstore, where I hide from aisle to aisle. She selects only one item, the shaving soap I've needed but forgotten over a week. On line she goes still, gaze fixed in the distance. She is somewhere else, a beautiful stranger.

Then she tosses, runs a hand through her wet hair, and I'm transported back to the touchingly goony barmaid of the E-Z Lounge feasting on a cigarette.

The sudden weight of the years almost brings me to my knees. The drugstore expands, white posts growing farther apart, until the building is so large I can't walk out.

I have never left Annie's shoebox house, I realize. For me the black still writhes outside, Annie and I fucking against it, tiny bright points like our knees' reflection on the windshield of the car before I drove it off the road.

And all the while, unknown to me, we were building around this house another one, solid, spacious. The materials are Annie's balance and happiness, her barrio kids reading out loud. Even my acres of sensible, water-conserving native plants. Annie's father dancing her around the reception hall. The Herreras circling, wishing and blessing a child for us. The long planks of this Good House, as I immediately call it, arch overhead into firm joints, a spine of beams.

I feel myself gathering weight, density. Cautiously, I allow myself to inhabit this Good House, which surprisingly fits like my own body.

Annie is through the cashier.

Dinner, setting down her fork, Annie says, "I give you credit, bringing me to this life I have. If you're going to destroy it I have to decide which way I'm going to go on." I embrace her and we fall into a stately lovemaking unlike us, or me. We fuck like two cool mansions.

When I break off, Lou says, "O.K."

It's time for quiet, for Annie and me to sit side by side on the couch, talking a bit, or to take walks.

Though yet only "trying," we visit a natural childbirth clinic. Wednesday night class is a room of oval women in colorful, frilly getup, balanced like Easter eggs on cushions. Their minimal, angular males are strokes and serifs, letters of the alphabet on the verge of making sense.

A very young couple stars in the birthing movie. At first I mistrust the boy's open-faced charm—my integrity shot, I suspect everyone—but as the film progresses I understand his grin is a rictus of terror and helplessness. Still he never leaves the girl's side, or lets go of her hand, or forgets to coach her breathing patterns, even when her screams erase him. The pregnant women begin crying. The baby's emerging head tears the vagina. "Oh my God," I say, but the audience takes this in stride. The baby is out; the boy's smile hasn't changed; tears run down his face. The girl's piping is unearthly—"Where is she? Is everything there? Honey, count her fingers. Honey?"

After a picnic, Annie and I bask in an arroyo. Inches from my nose, a lizard poises against the rock. The animal has the same astringent, arid smell as the stone, the sand, the air, as us, and I begin with Annie. The sand grits against us as we roll. I squeeze flesh and handfuls of sand as if they were the same. Smooth, steady, we build into a hum, the common music of the place.

Driving home, Annie lolls across the front seat, one foot on my thigh, head halfway out the window, reminiscing. Either her father had once borrowed her belt for a tie or she his tie for a belt. "I can't remember which. I know the tie was striped and the belt was pink. How you let me blather," she says.

"I like your stories."

Suddenly, though the road bends away from the sun, I can't remove my shades. The harm I've done to Annie would be exposed in my face.

As the pickup scuffs through the desert, banging the wash-board road, nauseating emptiness rushes in me. How easily I could say, "Let me tell you about Lou. This is what we did with each other————" Annie's face would contort—"shit"—her fist ripping the dashboard, plastic fragments rising. In an instant our union would be gone, we alone in the dark, with only our need for each other. Where I always wanted us.

But this idea, like Lou, is past. Though stuck close to me it is slipping behind like a shadow. I must wait myself out that much longer.

Builders

The closest three weeks of the Terrys' marriage had been spent vacationing in China, when their son Marco was an infant. Euphoric new parents, Dominic and Ella were traveling in a land whose strangeness was perpetually revelatory. Trivialities such as intestinal parasites and missed trains were powerless against each routine daily miracle.

In search of an historic temple they had hiked a valley whose river bent through rolling hills, forested ridges intersecting plots of ochre, buff, and emerald. Terraces ascended distant purple mountains, hung with cloud. The trail ended abruptly; above them, cocked on a slope, the temple seemed ready to break into a stately, comical dance. They were still. Marco stopped shifting in Dominic's pack. As Dominic and Ella contemplated the building, it became a Chinese guardian lion, the bristling roof its mane and flaring eyes, the arched portal a roaring mouth. They saw it exactly the same way at the same time.

"We have just been blessed," Dominic said.

Eight years later, lulled by this memory, Dominic was routing the site for his family's new house, preparatory to laying the foundation, when the tractor blade struck a subterranean boulder. The machine hopped, throwing him clear except for a hand and foot still gripping the seat. Lurching right, the tractor was sliding down the property's steepest grade, toward the ravine, blade spewing sawed-off prickly pear and cholla. The engine's stuttering roar, the torn roots and glittering mica rushing by his face, were an overturned world in which he was alone, his family beyond reach.

As Ella sprinted downhill, the bare ground tilted up toward her like a smothering hand while the runaway machine shrank to a Dinky toy. Then Dominic's broad back and black smudge of hair were centered over the controls again, the tractor veered up a slope, halted. Marco, eight years old, sobbed behind Ella.

"If I'd thought I was going to die," Dominic said later, "I'd've jumped off." He gave what Ella called his "pillaging Tartar" grin, upswept mustache over big white teeth.

Ella grabbed his collar and dug her head into his chest. "I used to like that peppy male talk," she said. "It gave me a thrill. Now I just think of the big hole in me that you'd leave behind."

Dominic averted his face sternly from this remark, hiding his pleasure in it.

Ella's dash had brought back to her a night just weeks before, when she'd been in bed with the flu. Dominic had scheduled a critical business meeting. After putting Marco to bed, he kissed her good-bye, waking her from a horrible dream. The door closing behind him panicked her, and in slippers and bathrobe she chased his car down the street. He turned the car around, phoned apologies to his colleagues, and played cards with her all evening. Not once did he complain or tease her.

The boulder was solid granite, twelve feet in diameter. Already $90,000 deep into the house—the lot mortgage plus loans to cover fees, materials, equipment rentals, contractors—the Terrys paid a demolition man $2,000 to blast it.

Dominic had insomnia. Budgets and time lines could not be reconciled, no matter how his calculations chattered on, degenerating into nonsense, arriving at a ruinous panic sale or foreclosure. "I'm sorry," he whispered to Ella as she slept. He felt like bursting from the house, never facing her or Marco again. Abruptly he padded into Marco's room and lay beside him. The boy's fingers curled into the sheet as if holding it down against a strong wind. His skin was warm. Cuddling Marco's shoulder, Dominic let the child's regular breathing scatter his thoughts, until the solution came to him, and he dozed.

"Here's what I'm thinking," Dominic said the next morning, over breakfast. Grandpa Harry would lend them his Airstream. Giving up their rented home and moving onto the lot would save $850 a month, plus putting the work site at their front door. "It would be just a little while. Like camping."

"Cool," Marco said. Dominic was touched by his implicit trust.

"We can do scientific explorations in the desert," Ella told Marco.

The tightness left Dominic's shoulders.

Eighty-thou-a-year Okies, what a stitch, Ella thought, as Dominic and Marco bounded down the hall on all fours, playing dinosaur rodeo. She was contented enough with the rental, its tall shade trees ringing the pool, and the years of accumulated furniture and knickknacks inside. But for Dominic's sake she'd talked up the new house. She decided to consider the Airstream an adventure. Anyway, it probably was inescapable.

Since Marco's entering first grade two years before, Ella had taught in the child-care program at his school, her first job since he was born. She marveled at the way her equable, deliberate sense of play kept the class ordered and happy. But the pay was poor.

When Ella had questioned the "gaudiness" of Dominic's plans —the expensive architect had been hired less to consult than to ratify—he replied, "Because we can afford it."

A 2,800-square-foot rectangle provided mass. Airiness was evoked by the steeply pitched roof ending in drolly flipped-up eaves. Centered beneath, the peaked porch roof risked clutter, the architect said, but successfully. Dominic was serenely loyal to his design; he had dreamed it, waking to scribble the plans in a notebook.

In fact, they couldn't afford it. Dominic's salary as a sales rep for high-tech medical equipment was pegged to a year-long market plan, his earnings increasing as goals were met. Dependent on big-ticket items such as Magnetic Resonance Imaging (MRI), which sold for as much as $2 million, his income could range from the mid-five digits into the solid six. But a citizens' initiative to cap health-care costs had paralyzed hospital investment in Dominic's territory, southern Arizona and part of Phoenix. Meanwhile, it was September, the house two months behind schedule. Because the Terrys themselves, not licensed contractors, were doing most of the construction, banks refused to lend more money.

Moving halted construction again. The night they occupied the tiny Airstream, Dominic bought champagne. "We're a race of giants," he said. "Our elbows and heads could go right through the wall."

The cement mixer rumbled up their hilltop site like a determined insect, inched backward to insert its long chute into the footing forms, and deposited eight yards of wet concrete, a shallow moat around the bare plot. Grim with delight, Dominic stormed up and down the trenches, directing and exhorting, raking the gray pudding into corners, smoothing it with a two-by-four.

Harry, Dominic's father, slapped the board aside. "Enough diddling the gravel. Gravel in your concrete's got to stay distributed even."

Though late October, it was hot. Sweat stung Dominic's eyes. The rhythm of his work absorbed sound; the mixer's steady clunk, the crew's shouts, the footsteps and scraping of tools were swallowed by the silence of his movement. In disorderly unison the Terrys wielded rakes and trowels, Marco flailing, Ella a lean angle, Harry prancing on spindly legs. Dominic's bulky shadow circulated among them.

When Dominic thought back to this moment, it existed outside time, in perfect balance like the bubble in a level.

"I want to punch Harry, the way he talks to you," Ella said later that afternoon. "At least when your mother was alive there was a courtliness to him."

They were sharing a jug of water in the Airstream's alleged kitchen, Dominic wedged between the formica table and the meagerly upholstered bench, knees spread wide.

"You're referring to the incident of the rebar," he responded.

"That. The two-by-four today. All the time."

Unknown to Harry, Dominic had purchased rebar for the footings cut-rate from a construction site. Days before, while laying the metal sticks in the trench, Harry had noticed powdery rust. He'd scorched Dominic for that one, but said let the inspection go through anyway; the contamination was almost imperceptible. The inspector, if he even looked that closely, should let it pass, at worst have Dominic wire-brush it.

Instead, the inspector ordered Dominic to rip out the entire rebar job—two parallel circuits of half-inch steel, twenty-foot lengths wired together, vertical sticks every four feet—and replace it. Though Dominic was itching to hurl each stick into the gulley, the presence of his family made him stack them in maniacally neat piles. He'd torn out the east side when Harry arrived.

"What in this fucking world of shit are you doing?" Harry asked calmly.

Dominic told him. "Nice call on the inspection."

"Oh my God, he got you." Laughing, Harry flung his cap to the ground and did a frisky goat-dance on it. "That inspector's playing with you. He knows you don't know shit. Half a day, a

blaster cleans off that rust, nobody can say nothing. Don't you see? You bent over for him today, he's going to ream your ass twice as hard next time. You're his toy now."

Dominic's straight-arm to Harry's chest wilted into a grab of the old man's shirt front. "My family doesn't have to hear this sewer mouth," he said raggedly, releasing Harry, who stumbled backward.

Harry turned to Ella and Marco. His face fell. "I'm sorry. I'm way out of line." He walked with Dominic, muttering, "Geez, Dom, I'm a falling-apart old crazy." Harry rented the blaster out of his own pocket. The rebar passed.

"It's the dialect of the American builder," Dominic explained to Ella. "I call it Fuckshitfaggot."

"It's personal. It's vicious."

"Man, I just blow it off. I go somewhere in my head, I don't hear it. I make twice as much in a bad year as he did in his best. And with Mom gone he's alone, and meanwhile look at us together, building this house."

Spraying the concrete with "monkey blood" sealer, Dominic and Harry tramped over a freshly-poured slab that for the first time defined the space as a house.

"Not bad for a fat-ass hustler and his broken-down dad who hasn't lifted a finger to a house in thirty years," Harry said. He'd worked construction two decades before buying the Quick Spot deli, later incorporated into a shopping center, outside Passaic.

Rooms sprang up under Dominic's feet. He called over Ella and Marco. "Look." He paced off the den. "Breakfast nook," a wall of glass block. "Fireplace. Marco, your room. The Roman baths," he intoned to Ella—a huge sunken tub. The Terrys stopped still. They heard birds. The mountains were immovable, and the only purpose of the white clouds steaming over their peaks was to cast quiet and awe.

"Mom, your bottom wiggles sometimes even when you're standing still," Marco observed. Ella was fluffing her hair at the mirror, in a short nightshirt.

"Don't I know," Dominic said, rolling the hem between his fingers.

Ella leaned her chin on his shoulder. In bed she used everything, nails, knees. Yet during sex her dominant sensation was peace. The louder she grunted, straining with him, the more tranquility enveloped her.

Dominic could say his marriage was beginning to stand alongside that of his parents, Harry and Bernice. They had remained passionate toward each other until Bernice's death two years before, when Harry left Jersey and followed Dominic to Tucson. "My mom and dad had the greatest love," Dominic said. Still, as he now discussed with his brothers and sister, the children at times had felt incidental to this central marital drama. The master bedroom, for instance, had been off limits to them except through knocking and waiting, if then.

In contrast, Dominic and Ella never closed their door, their bedroom the hub of weekend mornings where breakfast was eaten, the newspaper dawdled over while Marco's plastic dinosaurs played baseball, Jurassic versus Cretaceous.

In Dominic's floor plan for the new house, Marco's bedroom still adjoined theirs. When they'd completed the house, another child was possible. Ella was thirty-five, Dominic forty-one. They'd been married nine years.

December was the wettest on record. As Dominic made a two-week circuit of Phoenix, then Yuma, finally a *Tohono O'odham* reservation medical complex, the few spindles of framing the Terrys had erected gently warped.

Though eager for his homecomings, Dominic sabotaged them, as if Ella were to blame for his absence. They were celebrating his arrival with lunch at Denny's. "Occupational hazard,"

Dominic murmured as the waitress's straining bosom almost dipped into their soup. Ella was small-breasted. "What 'lungs'," Dominic breathed reverentially when the girl had retreated. "Chairwoman of the American Lung Association. Only a titular post, of course."

"Don't you go and be a cliché, hon. Oogle women with wooden legs or something," Ella drawled. Talking Southern warned Dominic with her dangerous past. Drooping eyelids, full lips, and a gap between her top front teeth gave her a look of guilty carnality. Seven years she'd partied toward her degree at the University of Virginia. Once a man she'd met on the train took her to New Orleans during finals week. He was bisexual, with a big, black lover who was the mayor's chief of staff. Years before AIDS, thank God, Ella thought.

That night Dominic curled toward Ella and stroked her thigh. His backside hung into space; the Airstream's bed wasn't designed for big people.

From Marco's bed, the kitchen bench a few feet away, Dominic and Ella heard his pages turning, the crackle as sharp as if it were between them.

"It's too gruesome perverse," Ella whispered. "He's not a baby any more." Dominic's hand dropped away.

Hurt and resentful since lunch, Ella took satisfaction in denying him but then couldn't sleep for wanting him.

Their first month in the Airstream, Dominic's internal clock had faithfully awakened him around midnight so they could make love. But after two weeks on the road, he knew he'd sleep through. Failing to make love for too long made them crabby with each other.

Felling the warped two-by-fours and toenailing new studs to the sole-plate, all Saturday and Sunday, they caved in against together at nightfall, unconscious.

Monday morning they attempted sex standing up in the coffin-sized shower stall, nozzle spraying (what passed for) full blast.

"Houdini wasn't much," Dominic panted. "All he did was get out." The pounded, groaning metal brought Marco running.

By mid-week Dominic and Ella were barely speaking.

Ella's day in the school portable had glided like a canoe, a flick of the paddle here, corrective drag there propelling a total of forty-two children, four aides, and six activity centers toward the sated contentment she believed was the entitlement of every soul on this earth. Marco joined her after 2:30, another reason the job was indispensable.

As a climax Ella was offering Messy Media, a potpourri of gluey pasta, mud, paints, papier-mâché, food coloring, and shaving cream. Swabbing purple suds from Marco's jaw, she found Harry at her elbow.

"I was too excited to wait, I had to tell you," Harry said, touching her arm. "Can you come?"

His presence thoroughly disoriented her. Harry, who had never visited the school, was scarcely taller than some of the sixth graders, though leather-skinned, with glinty gray eyes.

"Grandpa!" Displaying his shaving cream whale, Marco left purple handprints on Harry's leather tool belt.

Harry waved off Ella's rag. "It's fine, it's an improvement," he said, lifting Marco into his arms. Leaving her aide to supervise cleanup, Ella followed them to the parking lot, where a trailer stacked with fragrant lumber was hitched to Harry's ten-year-old silver Continental.

"Get a load of your new kitchen," Harry said. "By the time Himself is back from the wars, we've framed the sucker. You and me." Once again Dominic was in Phoenix, trying to close on the most promising lead in weeks, a cardiac lab.

"I know Dominic wants to be here for every minute of this house," Ella objected, cheered by her firm declaration. The past weeks she'd felt so removed from Dominic, she'd be hard put to say what he did want—sardines in his cereal? A trip to Lithuania? A girlfriend of another race?

"What a burden," Harry said. "Not to mention, if he's gone all the time breaking his neck to make money for the house, when does the house get built? Just my opinion, but Himself could use a happy surprise, for a change, instead of the other kind."

The thought of building Dominic a gift made Ella almost tearful, her first acknowledgment of loneliness. Saturday morning found her deforming nails and cramping her arm with lunging hammer blows while Harry chalked off stud spacing and sawed the lumber, which Marco brought to Ella.

The duet of Ella's sporadic rapping, "like a retarded woodpecker," she said, punctuated by whining bursts from Harry's saw, was unexpectedly pleasing. And when she and Harry actually raised a section of wall, nailing and bracing it in place, Ella felt a quickening of triumph. The city, yellowed by smog, sprawled well below. Thickets of saguaro and palo verde separated the imposing dimensions of their emerging house from the nearest neighbor. The Terrys were a foothills family.

Rejecting the emotion as unfitting, Ella returned quickly to work, to dispel it.

"I know how you love Dom," she began carefully, over lunch. Between the cold, gradually numbing when she sat still, and the stiffness from hammering, her fingers barely could hold the sandwich. "Why do you treat him the way you do?"

"Bernice"—Harry's voice still dipped huskily, speaking his wife's name—"Bernice and me agreed on most things, and one was that Dom needed pegging down. He gets swellheaded. He was the only one of us went to college, you know—I sent him. I was proud of him. We all were. But he had to set himself apart. That was the cost." While the other boys and even their sister helped out at the Quick Spot deli, weekends and after school, "not Himself."

"Studying."

"He was studying, yes." Harry laughed. "And going to the movies. Or taking the train to New York. I guess Bernice and me invented Tough Love before there was a name for it. Course I go too far. Parents always like to believe they do everything for a reason, in the children's best interest." Harry looked down. Ella thought he would have said more, but Marco returned from his explorations with a snakeskin wrapped around his head, and in the uproar and subsequent laughter the conversation was lost.

With Dominic due home Sunday evening, Harry and Ella had enclosed the kitchen in its timber skeleton with hours to spare. Harry smoothed Ella's hammering stroke, perched over her shoulder, hand alongside hers on the shaft, but without so much as grazing her. These attentions made Ella feel amorphously voluptuous. She was reminded of the Gibson girl in batting stance, frilly bustled behind tilted skyward as she leaned across home plate, whose picture had hung over her hometown soda fountain.

The reaction scared her, and in the next moment made her grateful it was only Harry who had provoked it.

Arriving jubilant with a sale, Dominic was furious at the kitchen. "Are you out of your mind? He's seventy-one."

Marco immediately took a stroll to collect colored rocks.

Guiltily, Ella extolled Harry's stamina. "He's the only way out. Not to mention converting me into something a lick useful, finally."

"I don't want him building my house," Dominic said. "He won't follow the plans. He'll cut corners, tinker with his innovations, leave surprises everywhere."

"How much longer am I supposed to live in this tin can?" Ella said. "Teaching, keeping up with Marco—who's been great—putting all my spare time ha ha into this house that might, *might* shelter a living body by the year 2000. Fighting off the creeps at the laundromat. Never seeing you."

Those last three words arrived like a rescue party. Dominic took Ella in his arms. It was such a relief and pleasure for both of them, not wanting to let go.

Although completing the house himself would have required the intervention of sorcery, Dominic slammed into the timber as if months could be alchemized into his spare hours. He framed before each workday and after dinner until midnight, by floodlight. On a Saturday morning, the cold breaking with the beginning of February, Marco joined him and Ella. Dominic was inserting blocking, chunks of two-by-four, at a corner post.

"Dad, I'm thirsty," Marco said.

"Just a minute." Dominic's hammering had found a rhythm. Three quick strikes played an ascending scale, like an African thumb piano, before the final whack buried the nail.

"I've been out here all day," Marco said. It was mid-morning.

Dominic was riding his efficiency with exuberant fury. "The jug's out," he panted. "Use the hose."

"That water tastes brown, and it's not cold. Let's get a slush at Circle K."

Dominic understood. They hadn't played a minute together since he'd been home. "Just two more to go," he said. Nails between his teeth, he centered the blocking with his left hand and drove one, two, three. Audacious with petulance and faith, Marco covered the protruding nailhead with his hand. The hammer, already on its downward arc, plunged through the nest of bones.

At Emergency the doctor set five fractures and hid the purple mass in a cast.

"I couldn't pull the hammer back" was what Dominic had repeated, packing the hand in ice, driving, briefing the admitting nurse. Sitting on the edge of the hospital bed, he explained to Marco, "I tried. I think I even managed to slow it down."

Marco's dark face was small in the expanse of linen. In an ethereal painkiller voice, he said, "I only wanted a drink."

The Terrys discovered the concept of overlapping time—the condition of living simultaneously within a project's schedule and its actual duration, the latter invariably longer despite allowances for the unexpected, which routinely surpassed expectations.

Thus, on a given Saturday Dominic mentally had completed framing an end wall, as promised by his timetable. Mentally, he was driving off the site to buy joist hangers for the ceiling, grab lunch with a friend, and pop into the mall for a gelato before lugging two-by-fours up the scaffolding.

In reality, however, having forgotten the window opening, Dominic was knocking a stud out of the end wall, then nailing the windowsill and header to cripple studs—while salivating at the taste of imagined hazelnut gelato, fantasizing conversations with his friend, so that he forgot to plumb as he went along, and eventually ripped out the lumber again.

This temporal incongruity could not be resolved. It was like the flawed porch corner, two floor joists refusing to meet square until Dominic finally hid them under decking. March passed. Occupying the house by summer, as originally planned, was inconceivable. Dominic borrowed from Harry to pay the roofer, plumber, and electrician. Marco's third-grade teacher tactfully omitted his penmanship grade from the report card. Whether Dominic took Marco to the zoo or squatted beside him under the kitchen table, animating the plastic dinosaurs, the boy awarded him the same sorrowful courtesy. He had never been better behaved.

An opportunity presented itself. The Denver rep suffered an apparent breakdown. If the company allowed him to commute, Dominic agreed to plug in immediately while keeping his inert Arizona territory on maintenance. The call came on a Thursday; Monday he could be in Denver. "Score some bucks, jump-start this shack," he said.

Dominic's plane vanished into the blue. Ella called Harry. "We have to finish this house," she began in a dry, tight voice, and was unable to continue.

"I don't hold myself above anybody," Harry said. "When Bernice and I were building our place, we were at each other's throats." He could spring for a contractor to stucco the exterior, but then they were on their own. "You've squeezed me dry, woman," he said. "I mean financially speaking."

Extending his legs into the roominess of the jet's first-class compartment, Dominic sipped his after-dinner liqueur. The past weekend he, Ella, and Harry had stood around superfluously, gaping as a crew armed with spray guns encased their house in gray glop.

Now he was recalling his prizewinning science project in eleventh grade, a waterproof synthetic fiber. After the awards assembly, Dominic had celebrated with a socially precocious classmate who served martinis in his own apartment. The friend drove him home past dusk, so late for dinner that the house was locked against him. Through the window he saw his family eating, heads bobbing, forks glinting. The rattle of the front door as Dominic shook the knob swiveled the heads around momentarily before they bent to their plates. Perhaps it was the wide dining table heaped with food, the interior lighting festive orange against the darkened house, that reminded Dominic of a parade float, his parents as Homecoming King and Queen with entourage.

Dominic walked the three miles to his friend's, where he spent the night. The following day his parents hunted him down in class. As they upbraided him in the hall, Harry and Bernice's hands joined convulsively, inching up each other's palms. Dominic begged forgiveness.

"Now that we've packed your dad off to Colorado," Harry said, "we're doing some building. Feed these to Mom." He passed Marco a bag of drywall nails. "Your dad has a brain the size of a battleship, but his common sense you could hold in your fist," he said, making one.

"He's got more common sense than that," Marco snapped. "It's as big as a watermelon. Bigger. His common sense could crush your whole car."

"Good kid." Harry nodded.

Ella enforced Dominic's one condition, that Harry be banned from physical labor. Instead he'd assembled and was attempting to supervise a drywall crew from Manpower. Diligent but inept, they sank nailheads deep in the gypsum, tearing the face paper. The line of installed Sheetrock zigzagged subtly. Mounted on scaffolding, Ella used her head to prop a four-by-twelve panel against the ceiling, thrusting with her neck, while a partner hammered. He slipped, dropping his end. As the panel spun Ella backwards, she instinctively collapsed her knees and crumpled to the plank, the Sheetrock fracturing thunderously below.

"Just the sky falling," Ella said as workmen stampeded in from every direction.

Week's end, Harry fired the lot.

Even hours past sundown, the captive June heat drove Ella and Marco from the Airstream. Crickets wound their little springs. Flooded with moonrise, the whitened hulk of the house was an absence, a subtraction from the landscape. When Ella peered inside, the empty latticework of framing gleamed like ivory, room after room. The random, isolated Sheetrock panels appeared as errors, stuck keys in this hymn to openness.

"When it was winter, I wished it was summer. Now I wish it was winter," Marco said.

"I know, sweetie. I'll get the fan tomorrow." Like everything else they possessed, it was in storage. Ella let Marco stay up and watch the snowy, rippling TV. School was out, the summer program just a few hours a day. After putting him to bed, she couldn't sleep. Those empty timber rectangles marched on and on like months.

She'd read the few used mysteries—her preferred genre—that she'd bought since moving into the trailer. *Newsweek* presumably waited in the P.O. box. Midway through Letterman, Marco came in. "I can't get comfortable. It's too hot," he said. He was looking at the floor, his tactic to keep from crying. Ella motioned him beside her on the bed. "Is Dad really coming back?" he said.

Ella explained that Dominic was working very hard so they could have a house again, one which would be almost too beautiful to believe.

"Some dads go off and don't even pay child support. It's like they forget," Marco said.

"Dad hasn't forgotten us," Ella said. She caressed him with a damp cloth until he slept.

In desperation Ella opened one of Dominic's professional journals. Though the text was chilly, impervious, she achieved a longing for him. She summoned the memory of the China vacation, the climb to the temple at—Hedong, that was the place. Dominic's sturdy calves and deep breath had led her, the cloud masses above breaking into the shapes of birds. The bundle of Marco swayed on Dominic's back. Ella reached to touch Dominic's hip, and almost fainted with love for him. The temple thrust up before them, its angles resolving themselves immediately into the lion's face.

Stunned, Ella recognized that temple in their own house, the symmetry of peaks and upswept corners of the roof, descending to the slightly busy porch overhang. She wondered if Dominic knew what he had designed. Three A.M. be damned, she would have called his hotel if they'd had a phone.

The next afternoon, as Ella napped, Harry knocked on the Airstream. "I could sit in the dirt and draw flowers on my toes," he said, "while my colleague attempts to hang ninety-pound Sheetrock all by herself. Or we could kick some bootie."

Until dusk Harry taught Ella how to dimple the face paper with a final hammer blow, leaving room for joint compound; how to snap-cut the Sheetrock with a utility knife and kick of the knee. They took turns bracing ceiling panels while the other nailed. One-handed, Marco stuffed insulation batts into wall cavities.

Ella's right arm was mush, and she had a crick in her neck, but the master bedroom ceiling was enclosed.

"Buy you a drink?" Despite his sweating, reddened face, Harry's body moved with the same loose economy as when they'd begun.

Presumptuous weasel!—Ella thought, instantly alert. But her retort slumped inside her. Having violated her promise to Dominic, allowing Harry to advance the house further than five men had the previous day, she couldn't be so puny as to refuse.

At a sports bar and grill, Harry dispatched Marco to the video games with a handful of quarters. Over pitchers he told tales of the Jersey construction industry, inspectors bribed, office towers sinking into the mud. Through every mob hit and union hall bombing, Harry scampered unscathed.

Ella even found herself chirping a verse of the Virility Fan Club song: "Harry, I don't know where you get your get-up-and-go. Here I am thirty-six, a teenager really, and you'll have to peel me out of this chair."

If there was any doctrine common to her mystery novels, Ella thought, beerily despondent, it was this: after committing your first murder, the next ones don't mean a thing.

Dominic, too, was revisiting the trip to China. Before catching the flight to Tucson, he bought a glazed ceramic lion in an Oriental import shop.

Ashamed and defiant when she met him at the airport, Ella hugged him perfunctorily. "God," she exclaimed. "My back. I forgot. Always sore."

"Welcome to the Bataan Death March," Dominic said, more harshly than he'd intended. Marco's right arm was still in a sling, a precaution. "My dad smashed it with a hammer, but it was an accident," Marco explained to a porter.

Flying in over the mountains north of Tucson, Dominic had scanned the foothills eagerly, as if he could distinguish the one white pinprick that was his house. Arriving on the lot, Ella's grudging embrace lingering on him like an ill-fitting shirt, he felt curiously disconnected. After Denver's bigness—his blue-glass office tower, huge hotel, acres of medical facilities, even the airport like a fortified island—he seemed to have disembarked in a Third World country. Ella and Marco were the rustic locals, he, in his gray suit, satchel in hand, the foreign dignitary dispensing the needed but resented aid package.

With scarcely a second glance at the house, Dominic was about to pop the trunk for his baggage when Ella took his hand. Pointing with it, she wordlessly traced the outline of the lion emerging from the rough framing. The Chinese figurine tucked in his suitcase, Dominic caught on instantly.

The anticipation of what was about to occur was so delicious that he lingered in it, approaching the suitcase with soft, floating steps.

Unwrapping the lion statuette, Ella threw herself on him, sucking, biting his neck and chest.

Long past midnight, when Dominic and Ella tiptoed from the Airstream, the moon had set. The lawn chairs cooled their bare skin. Ella rubbed her arm back and forth on his. He lifted her hand and held it against his cheek. He went inside and brought out Marco, still sleeping, to sit on his lap. But then, when he felt he should be most contented, he was disquieting himself. Did Marco, he wondered, love him for particularly Dominic qualities, or simply as father? Could someone else have stepped in and been just as much father? Or more father? And even Ella. Had she, at some point, just lowered her head doggedly and decided to love?

If he proved to be the wrong man, Dominic thought, at least his wife and son would have the house.

"Feed the lion" was Dominic's call to work the next morning, a full hour before overseer Harry, wearing a new straw boater with red band, settled himself in a folding chair, with a thermos of iced tea.

"My wife, the journeyman drywaller. She's teaching me to do arches," Dominic said.

"We can pick 'em, Dom. Women," Harry said. He steadied the gypsum panel while Dominic scored the back with a utility knife, preparatory to bending the curve.

After a while Dominic said, "It was awful for Mom to go so slowly, but thank God it gave us all a chance to be there." He remembered her shrunken, bright-eyed face still pleading and directing: Buy her a slip that didn't make her thighs sweat. Hold hands. The family obeyed. They surrounded the bed as if it were a palanquin that presently they would raise and transport to a delightful, refreshing spot.

Dominic remembered finding Harry crouched at the foot of the bed, in the dark, a mound barely larger than their German shepherd.

He set down the knife and gripped Harry's shoulder. The two men paused a few seconds, then resumed cutting the board.

"Grandpa Harry took us to a bar," Marco said as his parents were putting him to bed. He felt bad ratting on his mother, but the continued silence about Harry's activities gave him a sick churning in his stomach.

"Barhopping with the old man?" Dominic said.

"It wasn't worth mentioning, but I was going to tell you," Ella said. "My real crime is he's been hanging Sheetrock. I can't set a bodyguard on him. I'm gone hours a day."

"Let's get him the hell away from here," Dominic broke out. "Send him to Cancun. Money's coming in. A few weeks, we'll be contracting out this shit."

"Honey, I can't take any more 'few weeks.' I'll quit the school.

We'll hire us some men, I'll be out here all day with a bullwhip over them. I'll tie ol' Harry to a saguaro."

"You love that job," Dominic said, stricken.

"I love you. I love our family being together."

"You're punishing yourself for letting Harry work."

"Would you mind not interpreting everything by your piddling rules, even if you're right?"

Dominic grinned tightly at the numbness settling over his heart, in the place occupied by his house.

Harry culled Manpower for potential drywallers, Ella's assistants. The most competent, a Mexican carpenter, was deported by the INS after a week. Harry saber-sawed cutouts for electrical boxes. And Harry hung Sheetrock—but only when Marco was in school, at Ella's insistence. "Bad enough I lie without making the boy a liar for me," she said. She dug a trench for the backyard wall. Eighteen inches beneath the surface, her shovel struck caliche, which she'd break apart with an iron bar. Ella's formerly soft white arms were browned and lumpy with muscle like old mesquite pods.

For his part, Marco kept his mouth shut whatever his suspicions about Harry, an intuitively pragmatic choice. He and his mother depended on each other to get through the day, while his father inhabited the air, terminal-hopping between Tucson, Denver, and Phoenix.

If in his home market Dominic tiptoed a financial tightrope, Denver was the equivalent of seven-league boots. Hospitals within spitting distance of each other accepted bids for nearly identical multi-million-dollar imaging systems. Soon, Dominic thought, every school nurse would be demanding her own MRI. Logging four million in sales his first two months, he was flown overseas for seminars and conferences. In climatized capsules he soared from hemisphere to hemisphere, cloud-continents outside his window, the curve of the planet below. Drowsing, he jerked awake with a daydream: his family had separated. Marco would go with Ella; practically, that would be the result, whatever the custody settlement, because of Dominic's traveling. Harry would stick with those two, moving in as he became infirm. Ella sponge-bathing Harry's scrawny, sinewy body.

Dominic would remain plastered to the sky like a cathedral angel.

Sheetrock was hung, taping began. Frustrating to learn, the technique of "mudding" panel joints with compound, embedding paper tape, mudding, sanding, mudding, sanding, mudding the finish coat, was phenomenally boring when mastered. At first Ella's joint knife skidded fitfully, leaving a trail of blobs and gouges. Simply aligning the tape exhausted her patience.

Under Harry's tutelage, Ella learned the sensuousness of tools. With the pressure of a finger, the blade yielded to the slopes of a valley joint. The sander floated rather than rubbed, feathering the edges of a seal. Weight alone told her if she'd scooped sufficient mud onto the knife.

But the repetition, its tyrannical productivity, left her deadened and sour.

"I don't know why he bothers coming home at all," Ella told Harry over a pitcher of draft. "Himself." She laughed.

Dominic couldn't fathom Marco. One moment the boy was shinnying up Dominic's leg, both arms—at last—hugging tight, a familiar game. The next he was jabbing Dominic's nose and armpit with a T square while his father hunched over the floor plan. The night before, Marco had said, "Get your smelly feet off my bed" while Dominic tried to read him a story.

With a linebacker's build in hand-tailored fabric, and genial professional confidence, Dominic had his admirers on the road. He was accustomed to offers of dinner, and franker invitations. Since he and Ella were making love so rarely, he repressed desire altogether. Instead he gift-shopped. Saleswomen were infatuated with his gelded brilliance. The oak-framed wall mirror—so tasteful, sturdy but graceful, a hint of recklessness in ornament yet without ostentation. No less than style he appreciated comfort in choosing his wife's shoes—fortunate wife! The electronic baseball game, ideal for father-son weekends.

The presents irritated Ella. Dominic's bargain discoveries for the house, such as the antique wagon wheel, went directly into storage. "Honey, you want to stoke me, buy me a drywall crew," she said.

Soon, Dominic promised.

Ella was bored with her self-reliance. Requiring no will to maintain, it lifted her from bed in the morning, performed multiple duties, and retired with her at night. Unnervingly, this competence doled out even spontaneity and love. Her play with Marco was exactly inventive and silly enough, her rejoinders to him the proper balance of tenderness and instruction. When Dominic hired contractors to finish the house and Ella returned to the school, she pleased her students effortlessly. The flagstones she indifferently laid for the patio walk arranged themselves into a harmony that defied improvement.

As a warehouse assistant loaded bags of ready-mix concrete into her station wagon, Ella became aware of the man's hands passing inches from the tips of her breasts. The thought of his knuckles gently bending back her nipples occurred to her. Evidently her musings were forceful enough so that he paused, remarking, "This walkway, it would be some job to handle by yourself."

"I manage," Ella said.

Harry's voice, when Ella called him for a drink, was a coded mumbling she scarcely could understand. But he met her at the sports bar. Though she'd repeatedly invited him to inspect progress, it was the first she'd seen of him in a month, since the subcontractors took over, and his face was thin and pouchy.

Only when Ella relayed compliments from the drywall crew did he perk up, stroking his watered-back hair. Then he subsided again into his beer.

Though Ella fed him lines about his New Jersey exploits, he didn't bite, instead complaining that Dominic's brothers and sister had stopped sending anniversary cards since Bernice's death. "Of course, from Himself, some gilded tablets from the Hilton gift shop. Moses on the mountain."

Ella asked the proper consistency for ready-mix, mortaring the flagstones.

"Hell, I'll come do it myself," Harry said. Though Ella had seen him drink far more, the two pitchers left him blithering, sunk in his chair. He said he was too drunk to drive home. Contemplating the ten-mile round trip to his apartment, Ella agreed that he could stay at the Airstream. Marco was sleeping at a friend's.

The night air rushing in the car window invigorated him. "Hey bunnies," he called, as two jackrabbits strobed across the high beams. "Got yourself a real house in the country now," he told Ella.

Stretched full-length, Harry actually made the bed appear large. "Just your boots off is enough," Ella said, unlacing them. She loosened his belt. Rather than the clingy, semitransparent nightgown, she considered her one set of emergency pajamas, but they would be sweltering.

When she came out of the bathroom, changed, Harry's clothes had molted neatly onto the floor, leg openings of his Jockey shorts like two eye holes. Ella could imagine perfectly, between her sheets, the browned leathery body, penis lolling in its nest— was the hair still black?

"See you bright and early," she said.

"I'm not turning you out of your bed," Harry protested. "Put a two-by-six between us. I'm passing out, that's it."

"Good *night*." She touched the top of his head. Seeing in his frank stare that she was fully revealed, Ella could not leave.

She must suggest a cold glass of water, useful in preventing hangover. She must lean across the bed, adjusting the curtain.

Finally she lay down on the kitchen bench. The filmy nylon breathed across her body with the hum of the fan.

In the morning Harry treated Ella with the shy consideration of a new lover. She was mute with embarrassment, clumsy, upending a wheelbarrow of ready-mix over the flagstones, dropping a trowel on her foot. She couldn't wait to drive Harry away.

In the midst of conversation, Dominic would catch Harry shooting glances past him, for Ella. She didn't respond, Dominic noticed, but why would Harry expect she would? "I know you can't be having an affair with Harry," he said. "But why does it seem like you are?"

"That's the most revolting thing you could have said to me if you sat around thinking about it for a hundred years," Ella cried.

It was a bad day. Dominic had claimed he and Ella could tile the sunken tub over a weekend. But the several hundred thumb-sized cerulean chips, rather than conforming to the tight lattice flaunted by the brochure, undulated across the walls like shoals of fish.

Ella hadn't called Harry for two weeks when he happened by. She felt compelled to offer him dinner. They toured the house, treading earth-red tile in the den, pearlescent vinyl in the kitchen. The fixtures gleamed under the skylight.

"We'll be able to throw the switch next week. Dom's taking his vacation," Ella said. It was November, a year and a half after groundbreaking. "We'll paint together, trim, at least. Aren't those cabinets stunning? Dom has good taste."

Ella sat on the floor, Harry lounging against the sink. He looked awful, flaccid; he complained of headaches.

"I can't get over the feeling," Ella said, "that the minute we set the last pebble on the driveway, someone's going to haul the whole thing away, and there will be the vacant lot, and we'll start all over."

"Jesus Christ," Harry said, pointing. "The ceiling's bowed out."

Ella stared but shook her head.

Harry tilted her chin. The defect was visible as a fine gradation of shadow.

Ella cursed. "By the time I get the crew out here, Dom will be home."

"Screw the crew. I cover my own tracks," Harry said.

"No, no, no," Ella sighed, shoving his arms gently. "You've earned your bust over the mantelpiece already."

Harry's face folded up like an old glove. "Dom's going to know it's us. We hung this room."

"Dom scarcely remembers what state he lives in."

"He'll make it his business to find out," Harry said shrilly.

"Dom isn't that way."

"Pardon my French, but he'll bust my balls 'til kingdom come."

Ella couldn't explain, though she always remembered, the hardness that set into her then. Harry's very frailty goaded her. O.K., order the materials, she said; they'd begin the following afternoon.

When Ella arrived home from school, a T-brace of two-by-fours rose from the kitchen floor to a raw gray panel of new gypsum board. Bent backward across the stepladder, clawed hammer pawing the Sheetrock, Harry seemed to be crawling across the ceiling. Sweat splashed beside Ella.

"Harry, god*damn*it you come down right now."

"Sure." His voice creaked breathlessly. Dismounting, he moved the ladder beneath the other end of the panel, the last of four. He extended the hammer to Ella. "You do the honors. Whew." He wiped his forehead. "Hate to live anywhere else, some place where it doesn't even crack 85 degrees in November." Harry jack-knifed suddenly, crumpling against the wall. As Ella screamed, diving for him, he straightened, tried to push her away. "Hoo, dizzy," he said.

He was still protesting, jeering at her, as she drove him to the hospital.

Based in Phoenix that week, Dominic had made an unscheduled two-day side trip to a remote reservation clinic site. When he returned to the hotel, a sheaf of frantic messages from Ella awaited him at the desk. Harry's stroke had occurred not the afternoon he was admitted, but the following morning.

Ella met him at the airport. "Crazy," Dominic shouted, fast-walking her past the taxis, toward the parking lot. "Hanging drywall by himself?"

Ella was silent.

"So much woman you can make him twenty again," Dominic said, sliding into the driver's seat. "He used to box, too, you know. Let's hang a speedbag over the hospital bed. He can work on his jab."

"Dominic, let it go." She was crying.

Harry looked like a goblin, fleshy nose and ears prominent in his sunken face, his weathered tan paled to a dull orange.

"Papa," Dominic said, for the first time in over thirty years.

Harry's hand lifted in a wave.

Dominic adjusted Harry's pillows and bossed the nurses. Harry stared straight ahead, dozing intermittently. Dominic sat in the undersized chair, crushing his forehead into the mattress, waiting for tears. The inertness of his father's hand in his made him look up in dread. But the old man was gazing steadily at Ella.

Physically Harry recovered, but he cringed from Dominic in a defeated way until the February housewarming. Ella had installed the Chinese lion in a niche beside the front door. Harry told a number of the guests he was "waiting to die." But then he led the house tour, limping slightly, with an anecdote for every room. "Picture Ella squatting up there, just a thin plank holding her, and it's jumping like crazy as she drives the nails . . ."

Guests complimented Dominic effusively. His sunken tub was "a disaster," Dominic pointed out, the misaligned tiles slewing this way and that as if riven by seismic faults.

"You must be proud," a local hospital director insisted.

"I don't feel anything for this house," Dominic said.

The visitor looked to Ella, who shrugged.

When Dominic's company relocated the Terrys permanently to Denver, buying the house at a handsome price, Dominic and Ella were beyond regret, or even relief. Marco had foreseen occupying the house as the resumption of family life. Leaving filled him with shocked apprehensiveness.

The Terrys rented a spacious three-bedroom in the Denver suburb of Lakewood, Harry settling into an apartment three blocks away. He watched TV curled on the couch all day, ignoring Dominic's efforts to rouse him. Dominic couldn't see Ella without wanting to knock her down. Once again Marco instinctively protected her, creating diversions. He was suspended for tripping and injuring a classmate. Viral meningitis hospitalized him for three days, while his parents helped him to the bathroom and summoned the nurse for his painkillers. The doctor labeled his illness "opportunistic," with stress a possible susceptibility factor.

Dominic could not grasp how their efforts of the past two years could have been reduced to nothing, worse than nothing. It was as if a piece of opaque tape had been stuck over that time. The failure discredited them all, made them somehow unrecognizable.

He was destroying a nest of red ants in the yard. As the poison took effect, the colony's purposeful swarming deteriorated. The ants staggered off to convulse slowly in isolation, antennae and limbs twitching. He could not separate the image from what he saw in his family. He thought about the ants while eating and driving to work. It was worse than a tic. In search of relief, vaguely considering hypnosis or some drug, he went to a therapist.

"The lesson of the house may be that this is no longer the family configuration for you," the therapist said. "It doesn't work. Perhaps it did once, but people change, lives change. That's what we're not willing to acknowledge." She was blonde, about Dominic's age, wearing a severe teal pantsuit and chunky dangling earrings.

Dominic broke down, hands clenched between his knees. He scarcely heard what she was saying: "It's as if you lifted the shell off a turtle and found, say, a bluejay. What is this? It doesn't fit." The woman paused. Her gray eyes were kind. "It hurts," she said. "It's painful, casting off the shell. And freedom? It's not easy. The bird has to find food. Make a nest. See, I'm warming to my metaphor. There are predators trying to eat you, cats, and eagles. You swallow the wrong kind of berry and you get constipated." Dominic laughed a little. She smiled. "But at least you're one with your life again. When you move, your life moves with you."

Dominic took her hands, sensing that she was weak and unscrupulous. That suited his bitterness. Two sessions later, she and Dominic went to her townhouse. Stripped to the waist, she kissed him with pained intensity. Her heavy breasts, with their big yearning areolae, sank into his palms.

When Dominic confessed the affair, Ella was relieved, as if she were dropping to her knees to receive a long-awaited blow. But she kept falling, fast, and there was no bottom.

Dominic moved in with the therapist. Despite no prior experience, Ella applied for a job as office manager for a construction firm. "I just built a house with my bare hands. You think I can't shuffle papers?" she snorted. She was hired anyway.

For the first weeks, Ella was positive Dominic would return. Each of their conversations was incomplete, lacking his plea for reconciliation. As she realized that wouldn't happen, she cried for hours at a time, shaking, dizzy. Marco's reaction to what his father had done hurt and bewildered her. Instead of concealing the affair from his friends, he openly boasted of it. Yet he took care of her, drawing landscapes for her office and managing household chores during her depressions, when she'd sleep twelve hours a day. For him their bond was unbreakable, now that their deceitfulness had driven his father away.

At work Ella smiled at contractors and surveyors, bantered with associates. The competence she once had despised was her salvation. It was the narrow scaffolding plank that carried her safely from one Sheetrock joint to the next, over the plunge to concrete.

The therapist did impressions, including Nixon's Checkers speech in Bugs Bunny's voice. As Dominic laughed helplessly, she spread herself over him. "Republican cloth coat, ya maroon," she yukked in his ear, before sticking in her tongue.

Rising from bed in the morning was a daily battle for him. Though discharging his professional duties, he was indifferent to their outcome. He felt defeated by the slightest inconvenience, such as kneeling to retie his shoe.

"I know exactly what you're going through," she said. "My marriage broke up when I went back to school."

"I don't want my marriage to break up," Dominic said.

That sank in for a few minutes.

"You're ready to go back to your family. It's time," she said. Her chest flushed and her chin trembled. "I'm not a very good therapist. All I do is articulate what you already feel."

Dominic surprised Ella at the construction office, closing time. They could go out, he said. "I can't tell you how much I regret what I've done."

"Convincing," Ella said. "Did she write the script?"

"Somebody can make an effort," Dominic said patiently.

"Why?" She was still excited. They stood beside her car, close enough to touch. His size blocked the wind.

"Don't you want to try to work this out?"

"You sound completely false," Ella said despairingly. And the affair, which she had numbly accepted as a judgment on her, struck her for the first time as contemptible. " 'I'm done screwing this woman, so shucks, I dunno, I'll go home to Ella,' " Ella said. "Is that all the imagination you have?"

"I wouldn't say starting a round of finger-pointing is your best move." Despite the measured words he was suddenly heated, out of control. "This from someone who practically kills my father, slutting around."

"Now you're loud and clear," Ella shouted. She smacked his face. She was slapping him again and again, with both hands. "Now you're talking with spirit, Dominic."

"If he'd died then, you would have been the one with him, not me."

Ella slammed the car door behind her and covered her face with her arms.

Preparing dinner that night, she kept repeating to herself, "It's too pitiful that we've come to this." She pivoted awkwardly and the refrigerator's butter compartment knocked the salad dressing from her hand. She watched the cruet's descent to the tiles, where it burst, spattering her feet. She grabbed the catsup and let it drop, then the mustard, salsa, mayonnaise, fruit juices. Marco, running, saw his mother ankle deep in brilliant fluids and thought she had cut her feet off.

The incident of the refrigerator was decisive for Ella. She became parent representative for Marco's fifth-grade class and took him to Broncos games, fearfully expensive. She divided chores sensibly and enforced the schedule. For the first time she could remember, he told her, "I love you, Mom," and her heart was too full for her to sleep.

As she had done since leaving Arizona, Ella cleaned and laundered for Harry. She saw this as balancing the ledger. "You look lovely vacuuming," he said, tears in his eyes.

Ella concealed her weight loss under roomy clothing. Politely she discouraged the interest of a Department of Transportation engineer who brought her snapshots from his scuba diving in Mexico. While the house had failed the Terry family, she understood what it had given her—a stiffening, as from cartilage to bone, that she would not casually let go.

Dominic crashed with Harry. No longer shielded by the success of his family, he submitted to his father's view of him as quaint and hapless. Harry unwound halting reminiscences of Bernice in which neither Dominic nor his brothers and sister were mentioned. When presented with the wrong order by pizza delivery, Dominic stammered his complaint so unintelligibly that he paid up and ate pineapple-olive.

"I'll make more money this year than the President," Dominic told his father. He imposed evening game shows on Harry, pounding him in *Jeopardy* and *Wheel of Fortune*. Occasionally both men nodded off during *The Tonight Show,* waking in grayness, stiff.

Leaving for work one morning, he imagined his father drowning, blue face gasping beneath the surface, and Dominic's own arm shooting down, his palm on Harry's fibrous hair, pushing, the face receding in a stream of bubbles. Shoving the door closed, Dominic practically ran to his car, but the image bobbed up derisively in front of him.

Hating his father seemed to undermine the last meaning in Dominic's life. Yet there was excitement, too. He called Ella. "My parents were pathologically selfish," he said.

"You could knock me over with a feather," Ella said.

"Don't you see? That explodes everything. Even the house— I was building it as much against Harry as for us."

"Dom, I'm just about full up with the subject of your personal development." Her tone softened. "It is strange, not being able to talk things through together. But we'll have to do without it."

She did give permission for Marco to visit him on weekends. Dominic rented a cottage with a spare bedroom. The first night alone he didn't sleep or move until the alarm rang. For eight hours, his job would enclose him in the bubble of his talent, converting technical esoterica into market-plan increments. When he stepped out, pain waited for him with his overcoat. He never had conceived of hurting so much. The hurt was Ella, he knew, but it was too primitive to be named. It was simply a grinding against every moment. He tried to startle the hurt away by shouting, turning suddenly, but it was constant, unvarying. Opening a can of tuna made interesting ripples in it.

An anniversary passed: a year ago he had rushed home to Tucson and his stricken father, usurped house, unforgiving son, and alienated wife. That time now seemed an unattainable happiness.

At first he and Marco didn't know how to be together. Their closeness always had come from doing rather than talking, but Marco no longer enjoyed imaginary play. He needed answers for the loss of their family. Together they sought definitive responsibilities, lessons to be salvaged. Dominic wasn't satisfied assuming total blame. Nor could he entirely penetrate the dull, miserable fog surrounding Ella and Harry. He resorted to the house itself, as an implacable force of nature. "Like a boulder dropping on a frog," Marco proposed, grateful his father wasn't accusing him.

"Or maybe an MRI," Dominic said. "Maybe all it did was diagnose what was wrong with us."

They were leaving a movie, Marco's hands in the pockets of his gray coat. His face crumpled. "I wish it hadn't happened," he said, clinging to Dominic's waist. They dragged each other along the sidewalk.

Out of duty Dominic continued to wait on Harry. Disregard

for his father allowed him to see a disarmed, feeble old man, for whom he could feel simple sadness. Prodded by Dominic into regular walks, Harry perfected a downcast shuffle, but his color improved, and he began combing his hair.

Occasionally Ella would encounter Dominic there, coming or going. She was enraged with longing at his attendance on Harry. Never, she thought, had she risked the disfiguring shapelessness of loving the unworthy. Her son and until recently her husband were unchallengingly lovable. Her love seemed sleekly validating, like the vagina closing around the penis.

Eventually, the morning came when Dominic woke for work neither numb nor agonized. Despite the cold, he decided to walk. His legs drove against the snow, heels punching through the crust. He counted on their momentum to carry him where he needed to go, and he knew he could exist without Ella. Rather than detouring around a patch of ice, Dominic launched himself across it, skating on the soles of his shoes.

In the midst of his exultation he realized that Ella was the only woman he would want. He imagined her swatting his airplane from the sky with a big length of Sheetrock, and laughed, even though she sat astride Harry's shoulders, thighs clamped around the old man's head. For the other's sake, each of them had become the worst possible self, Dominic thought, he abstract, Ella corrupt. It had never occurred to him to define love that way, and he was shaken by the discovery. He could think of only one person with whom he could share it.

His watch showed time enough before Ella took Marco to school.

When Dominic appeared at the door, ruddy from the wind, Ella saw in his face what had happened. She had reasons and grievance on her side, but they buckled under love and she let him in.

They exchanged pleasantries, Dominic complimenting Ella on her swirling caftan, ignoring the gauntness it was intended to hide. "Aren't you going to kiss?" Marco demanded. They smiled at him.

"We're having hot chocolate," Ella invited.

"Take it outside," Dominic said. "The morning is so new and beautiful."

Bundled in down coats, they planted lawn furniture on the white covering. The bare limbs of the elm bounced in the wind. Once the three had imagined themselves as a house on a hill, dug into stone with the tenacity of a lion. Now they sat tensely in canvas-backed chairs stretched like slingshots. They talked cautiously, with encouragement, hoping for the return of pleasure.

Christopher McIlroy teaches English part-time at the University of Arizona. A cofounder of the nonprofit corporation ArtsReach, which conducts fiction and poetry workshops in Native American communities, he is also a consultant to the Indian Education Unit of the Arizona Department of Education. His stories have appeared in *Best American Short Stories of 1986*, *The Picador Book of Contemporary American Fiction*, *Missouri Review*, *Fiction*, *Story Quarterly*, *Puerto del Sol*, *TriQuarterly*, *Magazine*, and *Sonora Review*.